The Mystery of
The Missing Man

The Thirteenth Adventure of
the Five Find-Outers and
Buster the Dog

The Mystery of
The Missing Man

Enid Blyton

Dragon

Granada Publishing Limited
Published in 1969 by Dragon Books
Frogmore, St. Albans, Herts AL2 2NF
Reprinted 1970, 1971 (twice), 1972, 1973

First published by Methuen & Co Ltd 1946
Copyright © Enid Blyton 1958
Made and printed in Great Britain by
C. Nicholls & Company Ltd
The Philips Park Press, Manchester
Set in Intertype Times

"I'm going to buy some Easter eggs," said Pip, at break-fast-time. "Are you coming too, Bets? Then we might go and call on old Fatty."

"Oh yes – let's!" said Bets. "I've only seen him once since he came back from school, and then he was with Mrs. Trotteville and we couldn't say much."

"We'll call in and tell Larry and Daisy to come too," said Pip. "We might go and have buns and coffee at the dairy. Mother, do you want anything in the village?"

"No – unless you like to buy yourself an alarm clock," said Mrs. Hilton, buttering her toast. Pip stared.

"What for?" he said. "I've got a watch."

Bets giggled. "You mean he might get up in time for breakfast then, Mother!" she said.

"Ha! Funny joke," said Pip. "Anyway, no alarm clock would wake *me* if I'm really asleep. Besides, Mother – I've only just come back from a very, very hard term's work, and as for the exams last week, well I bet *you* wouldn't get top marks any more than I shall. I've not slept well for weeks, worrying about my marks."

"I suppose that means that you'll be somewhere near the bottom again," said Pip's father, putting down his morning paper for a moment. "Well, we shall know the worst in a few days' time when your report comes."

Pip changed the subject quickly – a trick at which he was very good. "Dad, what do you want for Easter?" he asked. "I did think of getting you some of that tobacco you like – and Mother, I suppose you wouldn't like a marzi-pan egg, would you, I know you like marzipan, and . . ."

The trick worked. Both his parents had to smile. His mother tapped him on the hand. "All right, all right, we

5

won't mention reports till after Easter. And yes, I *do* like marzipan. Now, do you want to finish the toast – because if so I'll leave you to it. Bets, remember to make your bed and dust your room before you go out. AND – please don't forget that dinner is at one o'clock *sharp*."

The telephone bell shrilled out as Mrs. Hilton left the table. She went into the hall to answer it and called back into the room almost at once.

"It's Fatty – he wants to speak to one of you. You go, Bets, you've finished your meal."

Bets flew to the telephone. "Hallo! Hallo, Fatty!"

"Hallo, little Bets!" said a warm, lively voice on the telephone. "What about meeting somewhere this morning? I've got a spot of Easter shopping to do."

"Oh *yes*, Fatty!" said Bets eagerly. "Pip and I were just thinking the same. Let's meet at the dairy, shall we – for buns and coffee. Say at quarter to eleven."

"Right," said Fatty. "Will you tell Larry and Daisy, or shall I?"

"We will," said Bets. "Have you got any news, Fatty? Anything exciting happening?"

She heard Fatty's laugh at the other end of the phone. "What do you mean? You surely don't think I've got a mystery up my sleeve already? Not a hope! As a matter of fact, I'm rather fed-up about something. Tell you when I see you. So long!"

Bets put down her receiver, and went to tell Pip. He was eating the last piece of toast and was alone in the room. "My word!" said Bets, eyeing the toast, "I never in my life saw so much marmalade spread on a small bit of toast."

"Oh, shut up," said Pip. "You wait till you go to boarding school – you'll know how nice it is to get home and not have to share the marmalade with about twenty others at your table. What did Fatty say?"

Bets told him. "Fine!" said Pip. "Well, you buck up and make our beds, and . . ."

"You jolly well make your own," said Bets, indignantly,

and went out of the room. She went up the stairs two at a time, feeling happy. Holidays were good – she wasn't all alone then, the only one going to a day-school. All five of them were together – and Buster. Fatty's little Scottie too – that made six.

Pip and Bets called for Larry and Daisy at half-past ten, and all four made their way to the village and went to their favourite little dairy. Fatty wasn't there yet, so they sat down and ordered currant buns with butter, and hot coffee. "With plenty of milk," said Larry, "and you needn't put in the sugar. We'll help ourselves."

Fatty was five minutes late. He arrived on his bicycle, with Buster running beside the pedals. He came in, grinning as usual, and swung Bets out of her chair and up in the air. Then he put her down with a groan.

"No – I shan't be able to do that much longer, Bets. You're growing too big! My word, you're a weight."

"We've ordered buns and coffee for you, Fatty," said Pip. Fatty sat down and gave a heavy sigh.

"I'll have the coffee. But not the buns," he said, to everyone's astonishment. They stared at him.

"Not the *buns*," said Daisy. "But – but you always eat twice as many as we do."

"I know. But I'm slimming," said Fatty. "Haven't you noticed my elegant figure?"

They all looked at him earnestly, running their eyes up and down him.

"Well – *I* can't see much difference," said Pip, at last. "Anyway – why ever are you slimming, Fatty? I thought you liked eating."

"Oh, I do, I do," said Fatty. "But the school captain wants me to be in the First Tennis Team next term – and I don't fancy hurling myself about the court in boiling hot weather if I weigh about eleven stone."

"I didn't know you were so good at tennis," said Larry, astonished.

"Neither did I," said Fatty, modestly. "But I was just fooling about with a racquet and balls on a hard tennis

7

court one sunny day last term, and old Dickory Dock – that's our head-boy – came up and – er – well – I hardly like to go on."

"You needn't," said Larry. "It seems a funny thing to me how many people think you're a Wonder at this, that and the other. Here I've been training myself at school for terms on end, trying to get into the football team or the cricket, or even the swimming, and I can't. And you just fool about somewhere and along comes the Head or the Captain or some big noise . . ."

"And says, 'Trotteville, you're the world's marvel. Do us the honour of belonging to the First Tennis Team,'" finished Pip. "It's not really fair. And you're *always* top of your form – and I'm never higher than ninth, and I have to slog like anything to get there – and *you* never seem to do any work at all. Gosh, Fatty, if I didn't like you as much as I do I'd loathe you."

Fatty laughed, and helped himself to a bun. Then he sobered down and looked thoughtful. "It's not going to be funny, though, this tennis business," he said. "I've sworn to get my weight down these hols. I can smash the balls over the net all right, and place them as cunningly as the next man – and I can take a cannon-ball service without blinking an eyelid – but it's this running about the court that gets me. I puff like a grampus."

"Well, you'll just *have* to slim then, Fatty," said Bets, feeling very sympathetic. "We'll all help you. What are you going to do besides cut down your eating?"

"I'm going to do cross-country running each day – or I might do it at night, when there's not so much traffic," said Fatty. "You've seen chaps tearing along all by themselves in white drawers and singlets, haven't you? Grim and aloof and determined – and usually frightfully skinny. Well, *I* shall be grim and aloof and determined – though I haven't much hope of getting really skinny."

Everyone laughed at the idea of Fatty being skinny. "Well, you've eaten *three* buns already," said Pip. "I suppose you didn't notice? Or did you think you'd start slimming after Easter?"

Fatty groaned. "Have I really had three? That's what comes of having hardly any breakfast. I get so hungry in the middle of the morning. Here, Buster, you can have my fourth bun."

Buster was only too pleased. He gulped it down and looked up for more. "Buster's doing well out of my slimming," said Fatty. "I keep forgetting about it, and when I remember I hand him whatever's on my plate."

"So *that's* why he's so plump," said Pip. "You'll have to take him cross-country running too, Fatty. He's all tummy."

"Fatty – you said on the telephone this morning that you were fed up about something," said Bets, remembering. "What did you mean?"

"Oh yes," said Fatty, absentmindedly helping himself to a lump of sugar from the basin. "Well, it's this – there's some kind of peculiar Conference going to be held here in Peterswood after Easter – next week, I think – and one of the members is going to stay with us – he's a friend of my father – went to school with him or something."

"Well – but why are you fed-up about *that*?" asked Larry. "You won't need to entertain him, surely? He'll be some old fogey who spends his days at the Conference, won't he?"

"Oh yes – but he's bringing his awful *daughter*," said Fatty. "At least – I've never seen her – but I bet she'll be awful. Mother says she's an only child, and that her mother died when she was two, so she's been brought up by her father. And *I'm* supposed to entertain her."

There was a horrified silence. "Gosh!" said Pip at last. "That *is* bad news. Either we've got to do without your company these hols., Fatty – or you've got to bring the girl with you wherever we go."

"That's just about it," said Fatty, gloomily, and took another bun. Nobody noticed, and he was halfway through it when he remembered that he was slimming. He looked at the bun in disgust.

"Why did you sit on that dish looking so new and curranty?" he frowned. "Well – I can't put you back – and Buster's almost bursting, I should think. Here goes!" And he munched the other half, still looking gloomy.

"When's this girl coming?" asked Bets. "I do think it's too bad, Fatty. Why should *you* have to entertain her? Why can't your mother?"

"Well, you know how busy my mother is, with committees and things," said Fatty. "She rushed off to something or other this morning and said, 'Well, Frederick, I know I can depend on you to make Eunice feel at home – and don't forget to meet her and her father on the eleven-fifty train. . . .' "

"Eunice!" said Daisy. "Goodness, what an unusual name. But look at the clock, Fatty – you won't be in time to meet them – it's eleven-forty-five already!"

"Oh, my goodness!" cried Fatty, leaping to his feet. "I must go. No, it's all right. That clock's fast. What about you all coming with me to the station and seeing what our dear Eunice is like? Come on !"

They paid the bill hurriedly and went out of the little shop, all looking gloomy. Yes – no wonder Fatty felt fed-up. Blow Eunice – she would spoil everything!

Eunice

They hurried up the road, and past the Town Hall. "Look, that's where the Conference is going to be," said Larry, pointing to a large notice. "Four meetings next week – and look, it says 'All Coleopterists are invited to attend.' Whatever are Coleopterists?"

"Colly-what?" asked Bets. "Fatty, what are these colly-people?"

"Owners of collie dogs?" suggested Pip. "Or growers of cauliflowers?"

"Or sufferers from colly-wobbles?" said Daisy, with a laugh.

"Ass," said Fatty. "They're ... hallo, look out – here's Mr. Goon on his bicycle. My word – I ought to offer *him* a few hints about a slimming diet."

Mr. Goon bore down on them, his uniform almost bursting at the seams. He was not at all pleased to see the Five, and even less pleased to see Buster, who immediately flew at his ankles. Goon kicked out at him.

"That dog!" he said in disgust. "Call him off! So you're back again for the holidays, are you? Well, no meddling in what isn't your business, see? I'm going to be busy the next week or two, what with a fair coming here, and that there Conference of colly – colly – er ..."

"Collie-dog breeders?" suggested Fatty, innocently.

"Oh – so that's what they are, is it?" said Goon, with displeasure. "Bringing a whole lot of dogs with them then, I shouldn't wonder. Dogs! As if we hadn't got enough running about in this town!"

He kicked out at Buster again, but the little Scottie kept well out of reach. "You'd better keep that dog of yours on the lead, if there's collie-dogs wandering about," he said. "Vicious, some of them are – and they'd make mincemeat of that dog of yours. Good thing too!"

And away sailed Goon on his bicycle, feeling very pleased at having ticked off the five children. Buster sent a volley of barks after him.

"Don't say such rude things, Buster," said Fatty, gravely. "Remember that other dogs are listening."

Bets giggled. "Oh, Fatty – whatever made you tell Mr. Goon about Pip's silly idea of collie-dog breeders? He'll be watching out for collie-dogs everywhere!"

"Anyway – what *are* Coleopterists?" asked Daisy. "Don't you know, Fatty! I thought you knew everything."

"Of course I know," said Fatty, wheeling his bicycle

along more quickly, as he caught sight of a clock. "Coleopterists are lovers of beetles."

This announcement was greeted with exclamations of utter disbelief.

"Fibber! Nobody loves beetles! Ugh!"

"Fatty – we're not as stupid as Goon."

"Think of something better than that, Fatty!"

"All right, all right," said Fatty, amiably. "I can think of
plenty of things. But that happens to be the truth."

"As if anyone would hold a Conference about beetles!"
said Pip, scornfully. "I'll ask your father's friend about
it!"

"Right. You ask him," said Fatty. "I say – that was the
train whistling – do buck up. My mother will be furious
if I'm late in meeting Mr. Tolling and his dear little
Eunice."

"How old is she?" panted Bets, trying to keep up with
Fatty.

"I don't know," said Fatty. "You'll soon see. Here we
are – just in time. Phew – that bike-ride was as good as
any slimming diet. Watch my bike for me, Pip – I'll go on to
the platform and meet father and daughter!"

He flung his bicycle against the station wall and ran inside hurriedly as the train pulled in to a standstill, the
engine pouring out smoke in a way that Buster could not
bear.

Fatty smoothed back his hair and waited to see whether
a man and a girl got out of the train. He soon saw a very
small man with a dark beard and large glasses fussing over
two suitcases. With him was a girl, rather taller than the
man – a stout, rather shapeless girl with two very long
plaits hanging down her back. She wore school clothes – a
dark blue belted overcoat, and a dark blue felt hat with a
coloured band and a badge on the left-hand side.

Her loud, clear voice came to Fatty as he stood waiting.
"No, Dad – we don't need a porter – you can take your
small case and I'll carry the large one. We're sure to be
able to get a taxi."

12

"Where did I put the tickets?" said her father, diving into one pocket after another.

"You gave them to me," said the girl in her clear, competent voice. Fatty felt horrified. Gracious – was this hefty, bossy girl going to be his constant companion for at least a week? He watched her take the tickets out of a strong leather purse, and then put it safely away again. She looked all round.

"Wasn't somebody going to meet us?" she said. "Well, I do think . . ."

Fatty didn't know what she was about to say, as he rushed up to the two of them, but he could guess. He smiled politely.

"Er – are you Mr. Belling, sir? I'm . . ."

"No – my name's not Belling," said the small, bearded man. "It's Tolling."

"Oh gosh – sorry," said Fatty, who had quite honestly made a slip. "I suppose – er – well – bells toll, you know, so I . . ."

"It's all right," said the girl. "I'm used to that silly joke, but my father isn't – so don't address him as Mr. Belling, or Jingling or Tingling – he just won't understand, and it's such a waste of time explaining to him what it means."

Fatty was quite taken-aback. "Er – I'm Frederick Trotteville," he said, and put out his hand to take the suitcase from Mr. Tolling.

"Well, if I wanted to be funny, like you, I'd address you as Frederick *Canter*ville," said the girl, and gave him a sudden grin. "No, don't take my suitcase, I can manage it, thanks. But be careful of Dad's case – it's full of beetles!"

Fatty looked down at it anxiously and was relieved to see that it was well strapped. He didn't fancy the idea of dead beetles spilling over the platform.

"I'll get you a taxi," he said.

"Put *Dad* into a taxi with his beetles," said the girl. "By the way, I'm Eunice – Eunice Tolling, *not* Belling. I don't want to go in the taxi – they make me car-sick. I'd rather

"But be careful of Dad's case – it's full of beetles!"

walk, if it's all the same to you. You can put this other suit-case into the taxi too."

"Yes, Mam," said Fatty, feeling as if he were under orders. He called the one and only taxi there and helped Mr. Tolling into it. He insisted on having his beetle suit-case on his knees. Fatty put the second one on the floor, and then gave the driver his address. The taxi sped out of the station yard and Eunice heaved a sigh of relief.

"Well, that's Dad safely settled," she said. "What time is it – about twelve? Is there anywhere near for me to have a bun or something? I'm famished. We had breakfast at seven o'clock."

"Er – well, yes," said Fatty, and caught sight of the other four grinning at him nearby. "Wait a minute, though, please. I want to introduce you to four friends of mine – Larry, Pip, Daisy – and Bets."

"Hallo," said Eunice and gave them all a swift look. "And I suppose this Scottie is your dog? He keeps on get-ting under my feet – can you make him walk to heel?"

"Heel, Buster," said Fatty, in a strangled sort of voice, in the midst of a dead silence. Buster obediently came to heel and sat down, looking rather surprised. Not one of the others could find a word to say. They simply stared at Eunice, and then fell in behind her and Fatty, looking at one another slyly. What a girl!

"Er – Eunice wants something to eat," Fatty informed the others behind him. "Pity we've just had our elevenses. Where shall we take her?"

"There's a tea-shop or something over there, look," said Eunice, pointing to a rather expensive coffee-shop which the children did not as a rule go to, because of the very high prices.

"That's too expensive for us," said Daisy. "They charge a shilling just for . . ."

"Oh well, *I'll* pay," said Eunice. "I must say I like the look of those chocolate éclairs. Come on – I'll pay for you all."

"Well – we've just *had* buns and coffee," said Daisy.

15

"We don't want any more to eat. And Fatty's trying to slim."

"Who's Fatty?" asked Eunice in surprise. "Oh – you mean *Frederick*. How rude! If that's his nickname, I shan't use it. Frederick, I shall call you by your proper name, if you don't mind."

"Er – no, I don't mind," said Fatty, signalling to the others to go away and leave them. He felt that he might be able to manage this awful girl better by himself than with the others staring and giggling.

"Well – we'd better go," said Larry, reluctantly. This girl was dreadful, but it really was fascinating to see how she treated Fatty. Why – he had hardly got a word in! And to think she was going to stay in his home!

"So long," said Fatty, curtly, and jerked his head violently to make the others understand that he wasn't going to put up with them a minute longer. Grinning at him like that!

They stood and watched Fatty and Eunice going through the shop-door and finding a table. They gazed while Eunice signalled to a waitress and gave a lengthy order. They watched two plates of cakes and pastries being brought, and what looked like a cup of frothy drinking-chocolate – yes, and one for Fatty too!

Eunice was talking nineteen to the dozen! She could talk and eat at the same time, which was bad manners, but very interesting to watch. Fatty looked thoroughly miserable. He kept trying to interrupt, but Eunice was like a steam-roller – and her conversation rolled over him without a stop. She had offered Fatty an éclair, but he had staunchly refused.

"Poor old Fatty – fancy having to sit and look at those éclairs, and remember he's slimming, and listen to that awful girl all the time," said Bets, sympathetically. "Oh, I say – look – he's taken an éclair after all!"

So he had. Fatty couldn't bear to sit there in dead silence and watch Eunice devour all the pastries. If he could have talked himself, and aired his opinions as he generally did,

16

it wouldn't have been so bad. In self-defence he took an éclair – and another – and another.

"Oh, *Fatty*!" said Daisy, still gazing through the window. She turned to the others. "Come on – let's go. If he catches sight of us, he'll be furious. We'd better go home."

Sadly they went down the road. Bets was almost in tears. "It wouldn't have been *quite* so bad if Eunice had been decent," she said. "But how CAN we let her go about with us – and yet we can't desert poor Fatty and leave him alone with Eunice all the time. It really *is* a problem!"

Fatty Escapes

Larry and Daisy went to tea with Pip and Bets that afternoon. Not a word had come from Fatty, not even a telephone call. But, in the middle of tea, they heard someone coming up the drive.

Bets flew to the window. "It's Fatty!" she said. "Fatty – in white drawers and singlet and rubber shoes! He's panting like anything. I suppose he's trying to work off all those éclairs!"

Pip yelled out of the window. "Come on up to the playroom. We're having tea."

Fatty went in at the garden door and ran panting into the hall. He met Mrs. Hilton coming out of the drawing-room with a friend. She gave a scream.

"Good gracious – what … ! Oh, it's you, Frederick. Have you come to tea in *that* get-up? Well, really!"

"Sorry, Mrs. Hilton – I'm just doing a little cross-country running – in training, you know," panted Fatty, and escaped thankfully up the stairs. The others were waiting for him eagerly. Bets gave him a hug.

"Oh – you're soaking wet," she said. "Is it raining?"

"No. I'm just hot with running," said Fatty, and sank with a groan into a comfortable chair.

17

"I thought you weren't going to start till after Easter," said Daisy.

"I wasn't. But I HAD to get away from Eunice somehow!" groaned Fatty, "and this was the best excuse I could think of. She talks non-stop – she lays down the law to me – to ME, imagine that! And she follows me about wherever I go. She even came knocking at my bedroom door this afternoon to borrow a book – and then she sat herself down by my bookcase – and wouldn't *go*."

"You should have *pushed* her out!" said Bets, indignantly.

"I should think that if it came to pushing, Eunice might send old Fatty flying," said Larry. "She's . . ."

"Oh well – if you're going to make insulting remarks like that, I'm going," said Fatty, quite huffily, and got up. Daisy pushed him down again.

"You *are* touchy!" she said. "Don't you let that girl get under your skin! You tell her a few things."

"I would, if she'd stop to listen," said Fatty. "I say – is that tea I see on the table? I'm so thirsty I could drink the whole teapotful."

"You'll only put back all the fat you've taken off in your running," said Daisy. "Still – you'll have to feed yourself up if you've got to cope with Eunice for a week! Pass him the chocolate biscuits, Pip."

"I shouldn't be weak enough to take these," groaned poor Fatty, taking three. "I know I shouldn't. But honestly, I shall be worn-out in a few days – and I shall be a shadow of myself – and I shall need building up!"

"That's what I said," agreed Daisy, pouring him out a milky cup of tea and putting three lumps of sugar in it. "But Fatty, seriously – what *are* we going to do about Eunice?"

"Don't ask *me*!" said Fatty, nibbling at a biscuit with enjoyment. "The worst of it is, Mother *likes* her!"

There was a suprised silence.

"But why?" said Daisy at last. "Mothers do sometimes like children we loathe, we all know that – we have to ask them to our parties! But how *can* your mother like Eunice?"

"She says she's so sensible and reliable and helpful," explained Fatty. "She unpacked the big suitcase and put everything away neatly in the drawers of their two rooms – and she went to the kitchen and asked Jane to be sure and not move her father's beetle-case, not even to dust it. . . ."

"What did Jane say to that?" asked Pip, with interest. Jane was not at all friendly towards beetles, spiders or moths.

"Oh, she went up in the air at first, thinking the beetles were live ones, but she calmed down when she heard they were dead," said Fatty, with a laugh, "and then Eunice went back to Mother and asked her the times of every meal, so that she could be sure that her father was punctual – and she offered to make her bed each day and her father's, and to do the rooms too, if it wouldn't upset Jane."

"Gosh – what a girl!" said Larry. "I can't see *Daisy* doing all that. No wonder your mother likes Eunice."

"She thinks she's the cat's whiskers, *and* the cat's tail too," said Fatty, absentmindedly taking a slice of cake. "She says Eunice has most beautiful manners, and will be *so* nice to have in the house, and is *so* sweet to her father, and . . ."

"Well – if your mother's so keen on her, perhaps they'll pal up together after all, and you'll be free to be with us," said Pip, cheering up.

"Not a bit of it," said Fatty. "Mother kept saying how nice it was for *me* to have a girl in the house, as I'd no sister, and all that sort of thing. And how we could do things together – go for walks – and go to the Fair when it comes – and I could show Eunice my shed at the bottom of the garden – fancy showing *her* that! I was furious when Mother even *mentioned* my shed. I was planning to keep it as a sort of hideaway when I couldn't stand Eunice a minute longer."

Fatty paused for breath. The others looked at him with great sympathy. Usually Fatty never turned a hair, thought

19

Larry – not a hair, whatever happened. "Did you put on that get-up and go out running to get away from Eunice?" he asked with a grin.

"You know I did," said Fatty. "Oh gosh – did I eat that slice of cake? I never meant to. I waited till Eunice was telling Mother all about the goals she shot last term in the matches – and then I murmured something about getting a bit of training done, shot upstairs and put on these things, and went out of the garden door like a streak of lightning."

"Let's hope Eunice doesn't think of trotting along with you," said Larry, with a grin. "She's pretty fat herself. It might occur to her to train too, and get slim!"

"Don't *suggest* such a thing!" said Fatty, in horror, and almost took another slice of cake.

"Well – what are we all going to do about it?" asked Daisy. "It's quite clear that we can't leave you to Eunice, Fatty – you'll be as limp as a rag before Easter is over. Let's see – it's Easter Sunday tomorrow. Then Easter Monday – we could all go to the Fair together, couldn't we?"

"We could," said Fatty, looking pleased. "It's jolly decent of you to let that awful girl inflict herself on you – but it will just about save my life! I'll *have* to put up with her tomorrow – but I'll arrange something for Easter Monday."

"When does the Beetle Conference begin?" asked Pip. "Tuesday?"

"Yes," said Fatty, "and Mr. Belling – I mean Tolling – has asked me to go! He has given me a ticket to take me to every single meeting if I want to go. Imagine me sitting there listening to beetle-talk!"

"Won't Eunice go?" asked Larry.

"No. She says she knows all she wants to know about beetles – and I believe her!" said Fatty. "I think she must know as much as her father – she helps him with his specimens."

"Ugh!" said Bets, and shivered. "I don't mind beetles

when they're ladybirds, or those dear little violet ones that scurry through the grass . . ."

"I don't mind beetles at *all*," said Pip. "But I don't want to be a colly – er – colly – what was it?"

"Coleopterist," said Fatty. "Ha! You didn't believe me when I told you they were beetle-lovers! I've a good mind to go to one of the meetings just to see what a collection of beetle-lovers is like."

"I thought Eunice's father looked rather like a little blackbeetle himself," said Bets. "Quite a *nice* one – rather helpless, you know – as if he might lose his way if he ran through the blades of grass. . . ."

The others laughed. A bell rang loudly just then, and Fatty sat up straight. "The telephone! If that's Eunice, you're not to say I'm here – see?"

But it was Mrs. Hilton who answered the phone, and then called up the stairs.

"Frederick – that was someone called Eunice Tolling," she said. "Frederick – are you there? Eunice wants to speak to you."

But Fatty was at that very moment climbing down the tree outside the playroom window. "Tell your mother I've gone – she *must* say that or Eunice will come along here," he hissed.

"Fatty's left, Mother," called Bets. "He's just gone home."

"Well – I quite thought I heard his voice just a minute ago," said her mother, surprised. "He must have left very suddenly!"

"He did, rather," admitted Bets with a chuckle, and went back to the playroom before any more awkward questions could be asked. She ran to the window. She could just see Fatty speeding out of the front gate.

"Poor old Fatty!" she said, watching him. "It's the first time anyone has ever got the best of him. Well – I expect it will come to a stand-up fight, sooner or later!"

Fatty trotted round Peterswood Village, thinking that he really must work off the chocolate biscuits and the cake that he had been weak-minded enough to have. Also, he was in no hurry to get back home. Could he slip in at the kitchen door? Eunice might be keeping an ear open for the garden door!

He circled his house and garden, and went in at the little gate that led out from the very bottom of the garden into the lane. His shed was near there, and he would make sure that it was well and truly locked as he passed. It would never do to let Eunice pry into all his secrets there. Then he would slip through the garden and up to the kitchen door and get in that way.

He looked at his shed as he passed, and tried the door. Yes, it was locked – and nobody but himself knew where the key was. Good. Now – was it safe to go into the house?

He crept up the path to the kitchen door, and listened outside. He could hear the kitchen radio going. Good – Jane and Cookie were there – he could easily slip through and upstairs. They never minded!

He opened the door quietly, went through the scullery and into the comfortable kitchen. To his utter horror Eunice was there, doing some ironing and talking to the two maids. She looked up in surprise as he came creeping in.

"Oh – it's you! Why did you go out running without telling me? I'd have liked to have come with you – I'm a very good runner. Don't go alone another time, I'll keep you company, Frederick! Please don't be afraid of asking me – I'm willing to do anything for you, it's so kind of your mother to have us here like this!"

"Er – I'll just go and change," said poor Fatty, quite horrified, and fled before Eunice could say another word. Have her with him when he went running? Good gracious what a truly horrible idea!

The Dirty Old Tramp

Easter Sunday was a glorious day. The Trotteville family and the Tollings went to church, and Fatty reflected that at least Eunice couldn't talk at church. Unfortunately she could sing, though, and almost deafened Fatty who had to sit next to her.

He was also very much embarrassed because of the surprised looks of the congregation at this unexpected addition to their singing powers. Everyone seemed to be turning and staring. Very bad manners, thought Fatty severely – but Eunice loved it, and sang serenely and powerfully on, basking in the stares of the people around her.

Fatty cast about in his mind to think how to get rid of Eunice that afternoon. He knew that his mother and father – and probably Mr. Tolling – would retire to have a nap. Could he say that he wanted to work? No, his father would certainly not believe that. Could he say he was tired and wanted to go home and rest?

"No! Mother will feel my head and see if it's hot, and think I'm sickening for something," groaned Fatty. "I think I'll go down to my shed. I won't tell Eunice. I'll just slip off down there. I'll take my book – and I might perhaps practise a bit of disguising. I haven't done any for ages – not since I went back to school last term."

Fatty waited until the grown-ups had retired to have a nap. Eunice was busy writing a letter. Fatty sat as quiet as a mouse in a corner, hoping that she wouldn't notice if he slipped out. But as soon as he stood up quietly she lifted her head and swung back her long plaits.

"Where are you going, Frederick?" she asked. "I shan't be long finishing this letter, then we'll have a walk or a game of something."

23

Fatty saw a ray of hope. "I'll take your letter to the post for you," he said. "Chuck it across when it's finished. There are two of Mother's I'm going to take."

"Oh, thanks – if it's not a bother to you," said the ever-polite Eunice and went on scribbling. With relief Fatty saw her blot the letter, put it into an envelope, address it and stamp it. He got up at once.

"Thanks," said Eunice. "I'll think out something for us to do, while you're gone."

Fatty shot out of the room and out of the garden door. He shut it firmly behind him. He was *not* going back through that door for quite a long time – he was going down to his shed when he came back from the post – and there he was going to stay!

He ran to the post, and then circled the house and garden till he came to the little gate again at the very bottom. He slid through that, shut it, and made his way cautiously to his shed. "Really!" he thought, "it's disgraceful to think I've got to skulk in my own garden like this!"

He unlocked his shed-door and went in. He locked it again, and sat down with a sigh of relief. Now he could be alone till teatime at any rate – and if he could be really stern with himself he could miss tea, and not go indoors until the evening meal. "I could say I missed tea because I'm slimming," thought Fatty.

He began to pull open the drawers of the old chest he had there, looking at his store of disguises – dirty old coats and trousers, torn pull-overs and cardigans – a butcher's boy outfit – a telegram boy's suit – and an old skirt and shawl and blouse that he had used when he had last pre-tended to be a gipsy woman!

He thought about Eunice as he examined everything. He began to have an uneasy feeling that she would not sit down quietly and wait for hours for him to return from posting the letters. She would smell a rat! She might even go and look for him!

And if she asks Mother or Jane where I could be, they'll very likely say I'm down here!" thought Fatty in sudden

24

horror. "Gosh – I never thought of that! I'd better dress myself up in something – some disguise, in case Eunice comes snooping along to my shed. I will NOT have her in here, pulling open the drawers, and messing about with all my things."

He decided that it would be easiest to make up as an old man. He had a wig and beard, and it was easy to paint wrinkles. He could slip on the dirty old flannel trousers hanging on the nail, and put on a ragged old mackintosh.

It didn't take Fatty very long, and he really enjoyed himself. He peered at his face in the mirror when it was complete with beard, moustache and wig. He drew very thick eyebrows, and grinned at himself.

"You do look like a rogue!" he said. "I shouldn't like to meet *you* in the dark!"

He put on the old trousers and the mackintosh, and actually put an old pipe into his mouth to complete the disguise. Fatty never left out any details if he could help it!

Then, chewing on the pipe, he sat down in the old chair there to read a book. He sighed with relief. Now he would have at least two hours' peace – and more if he could stop himself from going in to tea.

He grinned when he thought of Eunice sitting waiting for him, thinking up all kinds of plans, wondering why he didn't come back. Well – maybe she would be sensible and lie back in his mother's comfortable arm-chair and go to sleep – if she ever *did* go to sleep. Fatty felt it was very doubtful that she ever *really* slept soundly – she probably slept like Buster, with one ear open.

He suddenly remembered that Buster was still shut up in his bedroom. Blow! Why hadn't he gone and fetched him before he went to the post? Now Buster might begin to whine and bark, and wake everyone up!

That was exactly what Buster did do. He waited patiently in his basket up in Fatty's bedroom for some time. He heard Fatty going out to the post, and he waited with ears pricked to hear him come back.

But Fatty didn't come back. He had gone to his shed.

Buster grew anxious and impatient. He whined very softly. Then he barked – not a very loud bark, for Buster was sensible enough to know what Sunday naps were, and the house was full of Sunday – he knew that!

He ran to the door and scraped at it, whining again. Then he gave a sharp bark.

Someone came up the stairs at once. It was Eunice, of course. She, too, had waited and waited for Fatty to come back, and was beginning to feel annoyed. She liked Fatty very much, and felt that she had made a great impression on him. He was not rude and snappy to her as so many other boys had been.

Eunice had heard the whining and barking, and had been afraid that the sleepers upstairs would awake. "That's Buster!" she thought. "I'd better go and quieten him. I do wonder where Fatty is – it's too bad of him to be so long."

She stood outside Fatty's door and knocked gently. Buster answered by an eager little whine. He didn't like this girl Eunice very much – but he was quite willing for her to let him out of the bedroom. Then he would go and find Fatty!

Eunice opened the door and grabbed Buster as he squeezed out. "Sh!" she said. "Don't bark. Bad dog! You mustn't make a noise."

Buster was so surprised to hear himself being called a bad dog that he stopped and looked at Eunice to see if she really meant it. She took hold of his collar, looked into the room, saw his lead and slipped it on.

Buster was very cross. How dare this girl put him on the lead when he wanted to go and find Fatty!

"Come on," whispered Eunice. "I'll take you for a run round the garden till Frederick comes back! Hush now!"

With a protesting whine Buster allowed himself to be taken downstairs and out of the garden door. All right – he would soon find Fatty! He was sure he could smell him somewhere!

To his annoyance he could not get away from Eunice. She had strong hands and no amount of pulling on Buster's part made any difference. She would not set him free!

Buster felt suddenly sure that Fatty was down in his shed. He dragged at the lead and pulled Eunice down the garden. There was the shed – and Buster flung himself on the door, barking. Wuff, wuff, wuff, wuff! Let me in! Wuff, wuff!

Fatty was pleased, and was just about to get up and let Buster in, when he heard Eunice's voice!

"Bad dog! Be quiet! You'll wake everyone up! The door's locked, so Frederick is not in there. Come away, I tell you!"

Fatty crouched down in a corner in horror. So that awful girl had tracked him down here – with Buster too! If he knew anything about Buster he would bark the place down now that he knew Fatty was in the shed – as he most certainly did!

Buster proceeded to bark his head off! He yelped and barked and scratched at the door, and even growled at Eunice when she tried to drag him away.

"There's nobody *in* there," she kept saying. And then her voice suddenly changed. "Or *is* there? Perhaps someone is hiding in Frederick's shed – someone who has no business to *be* there!"

Fatty crouched even further back as he saw Eunice's face peering through the window. "Buster! I can see someone's foot!" he heard her say, in an excited voice. "I believe there *is* someone there!"

She went to the door and peered through the keyhole – and immediately opposite her she saw what she took to be a dirty old tramp, smoking a pipe. She gave a loud scream!

"What are you doing in there? Come out at once, or I'll set this dog on you!" she yelled.

Fatty was simply horrified. He couldn't *imagine* what to do! And then Eunice spotted someone walking along the lane nearby, and shouted loudly once more.

"Help! Help! There's someone hiding in this shed. Help!"

Then, to Fatty's utter horror he heard Mr. Goon's voice. Mr. *Goon*! What bad luck that his beat should have led him there just at that time.

The policeman lost no time in coming in through the gate. "What is it, Miss? Who's in there?" he asked. "Keep that dog off me, please!"

"Look inside that shed," said Eunice. "There's a horrible old tramp there – smoking! He may set the place on fire!"

Goon peered through the key hole and made out the dirty figure crouching in a corner. Then Buster suddenly went quite mad and attacked the policeman's ankles viciously.

"*Keep* that dog off me, will you!" shouted Goon, commandingly. "And you in there – you come out! This is private property, this is!"

There was nothing for it but to come out. Fatty had no wish for Goon to break down the door, as he quite meant to do. All right – he would unlock the door and make a dash for it – and trust to Buster to keep Goon away!

Two Exaggerators

"Oi'm a-comin', Oi'm a-comin'," croaked Fatty, stumbling to the door. "Keep that dog off me!"

"Here, girl – let the dog pounce on the fellow when he comes out," ordered Goon. "He'll catch him for us and make things easy. Look out, now – he's unlocking the door – the sauce of it, locking himself in like that!"

The door opened very suddenly indeed, and the old man inside rushed out. He lunged at Goon and almost bowled him over, big as he was.

"Buster, go for him, go for him!" cried Eunice in excitement. "Get him – he's a tramp, he's no business there. Catch him!"

Buster, mad with excitement at seeing Fatty again, leapt all round him in delight, barking loudly. Eunice and Goon quite imagined that he was attacking the old man, and were surprised that the old fellow didn't yell for the dog to be called off.

"Hey – he's escaping!" cried Goon, as he realized that the tramp was halfway up the garden, the dog still barking round him. "I'll go after him – you keep back, Miss, he's a dangerous fellow."

But Fatty had too big a start and was now out of the front gate and racing for dear life down the road. Goon marvelled that an old man could run so fast.

By the time that Goon had got to the first corner, Fatty had entirely disappeared. He had run into the garden of the house there, gone right down to the bottom, leapt over the wall and made his way back once more to the little lane right at the bottom of his garden. He and Buster stood there, panting and listening. Buster licked Fatty's hand, feeling very happy.

"They've come back – they've gone into the house, Buster," said Fatty at last. "Now they'll wake up Dad and Mother and tell them fairy-tales about an old thief of a tramp lying in my shed. Blow them –"

He slid into his shed, took his own clothes and slid out again, locking the shed behind him. He put the keys into his pocket. Then he crept up the garden to the kitchen door. He peered in at the window. Good – only Jane and Cookie were there, looking rather startled as they listened to something going on out in the hall.

"That's Goon and Eunice there, I suppose," thought Fatty, exasperated. "Well, I *must* change out of these things somehow – but where? I daren't go in yet."

He decided to change them under a tree – but first he peered in at the hall window to see what was going on. His father and mother and Mr. Tolling were all there, and Mr. Goon was trying in vain to get a word in – but Eunice was in full spate, describing at great length all that had happened.

29

"He was FIERCE, that tramp!" she cried. "As strong as ten men, Mr. Goon here said. Buster was very brave, he barked and bit – and the tramp kicked out at him like anything. Oh, if only Frederick had been there, this would never have happened. He would have turned that fellow out at once."

"Here!" said Mr. Goon, indignantly, breaking in at last. "What do you mean? If *I* couldn't get him, nobody could. I tell you . . ."

"A-a-a-a-ah!" suddenly screamed Eunice and pointed to the hall window, through which Fatty was peering, enjoying the whole scene. "There's that tramp again. Quick, Mr. Goon!"

Everyone raced out of the front door as Fatty neatly slipped in at the side door. He shot upstairs at top speed, and into his bedroom, with an excited Buster.

"Not a word, Buster," he said. "Not a bark, please. Just let me get changed!"

He stripped off the old clothes at top speed, and stuffed them into a cupboard. He cleaned his face, and removed whiskers, moustache and beard. Then he washed his hands and sank down into a chair with a sigh.

"Whew! What a joke, Buster! I wonder if they're all still chasing that old tramp. Disgusting old fellow, wasn't he? No wonder you barked at him!"

He sat and waited for a while but nobody came back, so he decided to go downstairs, and out into the road, and wait there. Then he would walk briskly up as if he had been out for a stroll, and pretend to be most surprised to see the others.

It all went off beautifully. Fatty strolled up with Buster just as a very disgruntled Goon came back with an equally disappointed Eunice, and a very annoyed trio of parents.

"What nonsense!" Mr. Trotteville was saying. "I don't believe there *was* any tramp there – just this girl's imagination! And you believed her, Goon! On a Sunday afternoon, too!"

Goon was red and angry, and Eunice was white-faced

and furious, but had enough manners not to argue. They suddenly saw Fatty strolling along and shouted to him.

"Frederick! Where have you been?"

"You seen a nasty-looking tramp, Master Frederick?" asked Goon. "Whiskers and all? He was down in your shed – smoking his pipe too. Might have set the place alight!"

"A tramp – with whiskers?" said Fatty, sounding extremely surprised. "Where is he? Quick, I'll set Buster on him!"

"That dog's already *been* at him," said Mr. Goon, exasperated. "Must have bit his trousers to pieces – barking and snarling. I wonder he's got any ankles left!"

"Well, Mr. Goon, I think we'll not bother any more," said Mr. Trotteville, firmly. "The man's gone – and we can't do anything about it. Come in, Eunice – you can't do anything either."

"What a thing to happen – on a Sunday too!" said Mr. Tolling, looking rather white. "A good thing you happened to be about, Constable. Tramps hiding in garden sheds! Was anything stolen?"

"What a thing to happen – on a Sunday too!" said Mr. Trotteville, beginning to look exasperated. "Anyway, he only keeps a lot of rubbish there."

Fatty said nothing to that. He was not at all anxious for his father to see what he *really* kept in his shed! All kinds of disguises, sets of grease-paints for making up his face, dreadful false teeth to wear over his own, cheek-pads to alter the shape of his cheeks, false eyebrows, moustaches, beards – good gracious, Mr. Trotteville would certainly have been amazed to find so many peculiar things!

"Master Frederick – perhaps we'd better go down to your shed and have a look round to see if that tramp took anything," suggested Goon, who thought this might be a very good opportunity of seeing exactly what Fatty *did* keep in his shed. Goon had a shrewd idea of the contents, and it would have been a real feather in his cap if he could

31

have poked round into every corner. Ha! He'd find a few of that boy's secrets then!

"Oh, I can easily look myself," said Fatty. "And I wouldn't dream of bothering you any further, Goon. You go home and finish your Sunday nap."

Goon went red. "I'm on duty," he said, "and a good thing for you I was too! If I hadn't come by when I did, that there tramp might have stolen half your things and set your shed on fire!"

"I bet he wasn't smoking," said Fatty, who knew quite well that he, Fatty, had only had an unlighted pipe in his mouth.

"You don't know anything about it!" said Eunice. "*I saw* him, not you – and he was smoking like a chimney – wasn't he, Constable?"

"That's right, Miss," said Goon, thinking that Eunice was someone after his own heart, willing to exaggerate to make a story more exciting! "A very nasty-looking piece of work, he looked – no wonder the dog went for him."

"Good old Buster," said Fatty, bending down to pat the little Scottie, and to hide a grin. Well, well – what a couple of exaggerators Goon and Eunice were! It was really a pity he couldn't tell them that *he* was the dirty old tramp!

The others had all gone indoors now, and Fatty decided that he had had enough of Goon and would go in too. He debated whether to bicycle up to Pip's and tell him about the tramp episode, but decided that he'd better not. Eunice might follow him there!

"Come on indoors," he said to Eunice. "It must be tea-time by now."

Eunice followed him in, and to Fatty's disgust she insisted on telling him again and again how she had peered through the window and keyhole of his shed, and had spotted the tramp, and how she and Goon had gone for him when he came out.

"I don't know why you *wanted* to go and spy into my shed," said Fatty at last, so tired of Eunice that he decided to be rude. Perhaps she would go off in a huff then. That would be fine.

"I was *not* spying!" she said, angrily, and, to Fatty's delight, took herself off at once. She marched out of the door and stamped up the stairs to her room. Fatty immediately shot out to the kitchen with Buster, collected some cakes and scones and biscuits from the tea-tray, and raced off again.

"Eunice won't come spying into my shed again today," he thought. "I can take these down there and eat and read in peace. I only hope Goon doesn't come snooping round. What a life – Eunice always about, and Goon popping up whenever he's not wanted."

He let himself into his shed, locked the door behind him, and sat down. He found his book and began to munch. It was only when he had eaten two-thirds of what he had brought that he remembered he was slimming.

"Blow!" he said, and looked at the faithful Buster, waiting patiently for a titbit. "Why didn't you remind me not to eat all these? Have you forgotten I'm slimming, Buster? Couldn't you paw me hard, when you see I'm tucking in?"

Buster obligingly pawed him, and whined, hoping to get one of his favourite chocolate biscuits. "You can have a cake *and* a biscuit," said Fatty. "But only to stop *me* from eating them! And I warn you – you'll have to go for a cross-country run with me to-night, to work off all this extra food!"

And so, when Eunice, who seemed to have forgotten that she had been offended, suggested after supper that they should have a game of chess, Fatty mournfully shook his head.

"Nothing I'd like better than to beat you at chess, Eunice," he said, "but . . ."

"Beat me! You couldn't!" said Eunice. "I'm champion chess-player of my school!"

"How strange – so am I," said Fatty, quite truthfully. "But I fear I've eaten too much today, Eunice, and I'm now going for an hour's run down by the river and back."

33

"What – in the dark?" said his mother. "Really, I think you are overdoing this running business, Frederick!"

Fatty thought so too – but the idea of a solemn evening playing chess with a fiercely-brooding Eunice was too much for him. Sorrowfully he went off with Buster to change into running-shorts, and was soon loping along by the quiet river, with Buster at his heels. What a life!

Chief-Inspector Jenks has Something to Say

On Easter Monday morning, just as Mr. Goon was finishing a large breakfast of fried bacon and three eggs, a long shiny black car drew up outside his house. Mr. Goon caught sight of it as he was about to attack his third egg, and his mouth fell open even wider.

"The Inspector! Now what does he want with me this morning!" thought Goon, and hurriedly did up his tunic and ran to brush his hair. He called to the daily woman in the kitchen in his most urgent voice.

"Mrs. Boggs! Ask whoever it is into the office, quick!" Just as he spoke there came a peremptory knock at the front door, and Mrs. Boggs flew to open it.

Outside stood a tall Inspector of Police – Chief Inspector Jenks, with keen sharp eyes and an impatient look about him. Mrs. Boggs showed him into the office. "Mr. Goon will be along at once, sir," she said, and almost dropped a curtsy as she backed from the room.

Goon came in at once, looking much tidier. "Good morning, sir," he said. "Er – this is an unexpected visit."

"Goon," said the Inspector, abruptly. "There's a dangerous man somewhere in this district. An escaped prisoner, violent and up to every trick there is. Known to be clever at disguises. Now – there's a Fair at Peterswood, a likely place for a fellow like this to make for. I want you to keep your

34

eyes open and report to me at once if there's anyone you're in the least suspicious about. I'll send men over immediately to watch whoever you report on."

Goon swelled up at once with importance. "Yes, sir," he said. "Er – would it be a good idea to go to the Fair *out* of uniform, sir? You know I took a Special Course at the Police school, sir – disguises and all that."

"Well," said the Chief, looking at Goon doubtfully, "you can try it, I suppose. Pity you're so fat – you can't hide that, and it makes you very noticeable."

Goon felt hurt. He looked down at himself. "I could try a spot of slimming, sir," he said, hopefully. "But . . ."

"Hm – it would take you *months* to get down to a reasonable size," said the Chief. "Now, here are a few details of this fellow we want." He laid some notes down on the desk and Goon looked at them with interest.

"Medium height, sharp-eyed, scar over rather thin mouth, which a moustache, real or false, could hide, may wear false whiskers . . ." Goon stopped, as an astonishing idea came to him. He stared in excitement at the Inspector.

"I saw this man yesterday!" he said, excitedly, and actually poked the Chief in the chest. "Yes, I did – whiskers and all!"

"Where?" asked the Chief, sharply.

"And he was violent, too – *very* violent!" went on Goon. "Kicked and flailed his arms about, and strong as I am, I couldn't hold him."

"WHERE was this man?" demanded the Inspector again, but Goon couldn't be stopped.

"And sharp-eyed too – eyes like gimlets, he had. And a moustache as well and now I come to think of it he might have had a scar under it. Bless me, if he wasn't the man!"

"GOON," said the Chief, in a dangerous voice. "Kindly stop gabbling and listen to me. WHERE was this fellow?"

"Er – well, sir – funny thing, sir, but he was in that Frederick Trotteville's garden, down in his shed," said Goon. "I was called in by a young lady staying there, sir.

35

Buster, that Scottie, he went for the old tramp fiercely, and must have bitten his ankles to the bone. Real savage he was, sir."

"Was Frederick Trotteville there, too?" asked the Chief. "Couldn't *he* catch the man? He's usually pretty nippy at that kind of thing."

"Well, if that fellow could have been caught, *I'd* have caught him," said Goon, huffily. "Actually Master Frederick didn't come along till too late. I'd done the dirty work before he turned up."

"I see," said the Inspector, thoughtfully. "I think I'll go along and see what Frederick thought of this fellow."

"He didn't see him, sir," said Goon. "I told you, he came along too late."

"Yes, I heard you," said the Chief, curtly. "All right. Study those notes, Goon, and keep your eyes skinned. That fellow has been seen here – and we know he's got friends nearby who might fix him up with some disguise. He's not a fellow who'll hide away. He'd take a delight in mixing with people somewhere and watching the police trying to find him."

"Ho – then I'll certainly disguise myself," said Goon. "Supposing I put on my . . ."

But the Inspector was already striding out to his car, and Goon was left muttering to himself. "To the Trottevilles' house," ordered the Inspector, and the big car slid smoothly away. It turned in at Fatty's drive and stopped beside the front door. The Inspector got out and rang the bell.

"Is Master Frederick in?" he asked, when Jane came to the door.

"Oh, good morning, sir," said Jane. "Yes, I think so. He was just going out. Come in, sir, and I'll call him."

The Chief Inspector stepped in and was shown into Mrs. Trotteville's pretty drawing-room. Then came the sound of hurried footsteps down the stairs and Fatty appeared, dressed in running-shorts and white singlet. The Chief looked surprised.

36

"Hallo, Frederick – in training for something?" he enquired.

"Yes, sir. Getting a bit of my fat off," explained Fatty. "I've a chance of getting into the First Tennis Team next term. Nice to see you, sir!"

The Inspector came straight to the point. "Frederick – I've just come from Goon," he said. "I went to see him to ask him to look out for someone for me – and he immediately started a peculiar story about a tramp he'd found down in your shed."

Fatty felt himself going red. "Yes, sir," he said. "Er – what else did he tell you?"

"Oh, I got a good many details from him," said the Chief, dryly. "According to him, this fellow was extremely violent, had very sharp eyes, like gimlets, and a moustache, probably with a scar under it – and Buster flew at him and bit his ankles to the bone. The tramp's ankles, not Goon's."

"Did he say anything else, sir?" asked Fatty, cautiously.

"He did say that you turned up too late to help him," said the Inspector. "Exactly what do you know about this violent tramp who was hiding in your shed? I thought you always kept it locked."

"You think I was that tramp, sir, don't you?" said Fatty, looking the Chief in the eyes.

"It certainly had occurred to me," said the Chief, looking straight back at Fatty.

"All right," said Fatty, with a sigh. "Yes, I was the tramp. But it was only a joke, sir. I didn't even know Goon was anywhere near. A friend of ours, staying here, peeped into my shed and saw me there, looking like a tramp – I was in disguise, of course – and screamed for help. And Goon came in, and I got away. Buster didn't go for me, of course – he was just excited to see me and leapt all round me as I went. Er – Goon exaggerated a bit, I expect."

"Yes. I guessed as much," said the Inspector, a twinkle in his eye. "You were extremely strong and violent, according to him – he quite thought you were the man we're after."

"I suppose – I suppose you wouldn't care to tell me about this man," said Fatty, hopefully. "I mean – I might be able to help. You never know."

"I'll leave you a copy of the notes I left with Goon," said the Chief, and he took a sheaf of papers from his pocket and extracted two or three pages from them. "Better not tell Goon that you know about this man – but keep your eyes open for anything out of the way this next week. The Fair's on – and there's a Conference of some sort on too – so the place will be full of strangers."

"Oh, thanks, sir," said Fatty, joyfully, as he picked up the notes. "Thanks a lot. This is right up my street! I'll do my best. I can tell the others, sir, can't I? You know they can be trusted too – we've done quite a lot to help you in the past, haven't we?"

The Chief laughed. "Yes. So long as you give the orders to the others, and they obey you, that's all right. But remember, Frederick – this fellow is dangerous – all I want you to do is to keep your eyes and ears open and pass on anything you hear that might be of value. You've got a way of picking up information – in fact I might almost say you've got a gift for it!"

"Thanks, Chief," said Fatty, pleased, and saw him politely to the front door. As soon as he had shut it Eunice came running up to him.

"Who was that, Frederick? It was a Chief Inspector, wasn't it? What did he want to see you for? Was it about that tramp yesterday?"

"Yes – mostly about him," said Fatty, guardedly. He wasn't going to let Eunice know what else the Chief had told him.

"Well – I do think you might have called *me*," said Eunice, indignantly. "After all, *I* found him – and *I* called the policeman – and *I* tried to catch him."

"Well – the Chief got all the information from Goon, I

38

expect," said Fatty. "Now I must start on my training, Eunice. Sorry to have to leave you to yourself."

"I'll come too," said Eunice, but at that moment Mrs. Trotteville came in, and, to Fatty's relief, made it impossible for Eunice to go with him, by asking her if she would mind arranging the flowers.

Eunice, always good-mannered with her elders, agreed at once, and Fatty fled in delight. He meant to go and tell the others the exciting news he had, and he waited until Eunice was safely in the garden and then flew to the telephone.

He rang Pip's number, but it was engaged. Blow! He rang Larry's and to his relief Daisy came to the phone.

"Daisy! Listen – there's a Mystery looming up!" said Fatty, delightedly. "A smasher! The Chief Inspector has just been here, and he wants our help. Can we meet at your house in ten minutes' time? We can? Good. Ring Pip for me, will you, and get him and Bets along too."

He rang off, smiling – but as he turned he heard a reproachful voice. "Frederick! You said the Chief came about that tramp. What *did* he come for? And what's this about a mystery? I do think you might tell me."

It was Eunice who had come in at the garden door with some daffodils. She had heard every word!

"Sorry. Can't stop, Eunice!" said Fatty, and ran straight out of the front door, Buster at his heels. He had meant to change back into flannels, but he felt that Eunice would probably follow him right up to his room and harangue him there about their "mystery".

So away he fled to Larry's, still in running things, leaving a very angry Eunice glaring after him. How *maddening* that she had overheard him on the telephone!

Larry and Daisy were in their summer-house waiting for him. Pip and Bets had not yet arrived. They were surprised to see Fatty in running shorts again.

"I say – do you *live* in those?" said Larry. "I'd better get you a coat. You'll shiver out here. The wind is blowing straight into the summer-house."

Pip and Bets arrived almost immediately, and the five, with a happy and interested Buster, held a most interesting meeting.

Fatty first of all told them the story of how he had escaped from Eunice the day before and gone down to his shed and practised a little disguising.

"I put on the tramp rig-out," he said. "Whiskers and all. So, of course, when Eunice came peeping in at the window and the keyhole, she got a bit of a shock, and yelled for help!"

They all laughed. "Serve her right for snooping," said Larry. "Go on."

"Well, who should come to her help but old Goon, who was walking down the lane nearby, on his Sunday beat," said Fatty. "So you can guess I had a Bit of a Do getting away. Buster nearly went mad with excitement and jumped all over me and rushed off beside me – and Goon and Eunice thought he was attacking me – Goon said he must have bitten my ankles to the bone!"

"But they *didn't* catch you, did they?" said Bets, anxiously.

"Of course not," went on Fatty. "Anyway, it happened that the Chief Inspector went to see Goon about some dangerous fellow – an escaped prisoner – whom he thinks is hiding somewhere in Peterswood – and old Goon told him all about the tramp he'd chased out of my shed, and said he was sure he was the prisoner, hiding there!"

There was such uproarious laughter over this that it was some time before Fatty could go on. "Do shut up," he begged. "You'll bring your mother out here, Larry – she'll think we're planning something awful."

"All right – but it's very funny," said Larry. "What next?"

"Well, as you can imagine, the Chief wasn't as idiotic as Goon," said Fatty. "He guessed at once that the old tramp was me, and came to tackle me about it."

Everyone gazed anxiously at Fatty.

"Was he angry?" asked Bets.

"No. Of course not. Can't I practise disguising myself down in my own shed if I want to?" said Fatty. "Of course I can! But, you see, the Chief had to let the cat out of the bag – he had to tell me about the man that Goon thought I was! And I pounced on that at once, and asked if we could help in any way. And he said we could!"

"I *say*!" said Pip, thrilled. "Then we've got another Mystery to get our teeth into. Well – perhaps not quite a *mystery* – but something very like it! Do you know anything about this man?"

"Yes. Look," said Fatty, and put his notes down on the summer-house table. "Here are the particulars. And here are photos of the man too – front face and side face. But he'll be in disguise – he's clever at that, apparently – so the photos won't be *much* good."

They all stared down at them. The man had very sharp, intelligent eyes under dark brows, an ordinary nose, and thin mouth, and over it, under the nose, a thin, curving scar. Fatty pointed to it.

"He'll have to hide *that*," he said. "And that probably means he will be wearing a false moustache until he can grow one. He may even wear a beard too, to hide his rather weak chin."

The man's hair was thick and straight. "He could wave that – or have it permed," said Fatty. "Or perhaps have

41

it thinned so that he looked a bit bald. You never know."

"Well – if he can do all those things to himself I don't see what use these photos are," said Daisy.

"His hands are a bit knobbly, look," said Pip. "I bet he'll wear gloves to hide those!"

"Except that plenty of people have knobbly hands," said Bets. "Our gardener has, for instance. Very knobbly."

"Has he any likes or dislikes?" asked Daisy.

"Apparently he is fond of cats," said Fatty. "And dear me, look – here's an odd thing I didn't notice before. He is interested in Nature, but especially in *insects*. A-HA!"

"What's the A-HA for?" asked Pip, surprised.

"Interested in *insects* – and he's known to be in *Peterswood*," said Fatty. "Doesn't that ring a bell, my dear Fatheads?"

"Oh – you mean the Conference of Colly-something," said Larry, remembering. "Yes – yes, there may be something in that. You mean, he may get himself up as a collysomething – a beetle-lover – and go and sit solemnly in the meetings at the Town Hall, while everyone is looking for him elsewhere."

"Well – it does sound a bit far-fetched," admitted Fatty. "But we can't afford to miss any possible clue. It might be the best possible hiding-place – meetings for beetle-lovers! Whoever would think of looking for an escaped prisoner there? With thick glasses to hide his sharp eyes. . . ."

"And the kind of hat and muffler and thick coat that Mr. Tolling wears," said Bets. "Honestly, I couldn't help thinking *he* looked as if he was in disguise when we saw him at the station – moustache and beard and all!"

"Well, we've got a difficult job on," said Fatty, sounding pleased as he gathered up the papers. "But we're going to have some fun! And remember – Goon is also on the look-out for this fellow, and whatever we do we mustn't let him spot him first!"

"Good gracious, no!" said Daisy. "By the way, what height is the man? Tall? Short?"

"Medium," said Fatty. "But we must remember that he

can make himself taller by wearing higher heels, or shorter by stooping. Inspector Jenks said he was very good at disguising himself. Now, we must make plans."

"Yes. Let's," said Bets. "And we mustn't let Eunice know a thing."

"She overheard my conversation with Daisy, on the telephone," said Fatty, frowning. "Just like her! She was very inquisitive as to why the Chief had come to see me this morning, of course – and angry because he didn't see *her* about the old tramp. Little does she know that he was only me, down in that shed!"

"Well, we'll certainly have to be careful when Eunice is about," said Larry. "Now – how are we going to set about this mystery, Fatty? Let's think."

"Well, it's obvious that the fellow must mix with plenty of other people, where he would go unnoticed," said Fatty, considering. "He probably wouldn't want to take a room in a hotel – or in a boarding-house. He would know that the police would make enquiries at all those. No – *I* think there are two places to look for him."

"What are they?" asked Bets. "The Fair is one, of course."

"And the Coleopterist Conference is the second," said Fatty. "I'm sure of that."

"But we can't get into any of their meetings," objected Daisy. "We're none of us colly-whatever-you-said."

"*I* can get in," said Fatty. "Eunice's father gave me tickets for every meeting! He gave Mother and Dad some too – so we can go to any meeting we like!"

"Well, *I* don't want to," said Daisy, decidedly. "Ugh – beetles crawling about all over the place."

"Don't be an ass. If there are beetles on show, they'll be stuck in rows in cases," said Larry. "Won't they, Fatty? As dead as door-nails!"

"Yes. But I expect that all that will happen at the meetings is that the chief coleopterists will get up and make long, long speeches," said Fatty. "They might perhaps chat together at the end of each meeting. It will be very, very dull for any of us whose job it is to attend one in order to examine the coleopterists to see if any of them resemble the escaped prisoner."

"Bags I don't," said Daisy, promptly. "I'd rather go to the Fair."

"Oh well – we'll *all* go there," agreed Fatty. "Actually, I thought we'd go this afternoon. The Coleopterist Conference doesn't begin till tomorrow, anyway. So what about a visit to the Fair and mixing business with pleasure?"

Everyone thought that this was a very good idea. "But what about Eunice?" said Bets, anxiously. "Will she have to come too?"

There was a moment's silence and then Fatty gave a heavy sigh. "I don't see any way out of that," he said. "Mother will expect me to take her, and she'll kick up an awful fuss if I try to get out of it. Blow!"

"We'll try and take it in turns to be with her," said Larry, generously. "You're the brightest one of us all, Fatty, so you're more likely to spot anyone like the man we're after – and if this afternoon you see anyone you particularly want to examine, or follow, or talk to, just give me one of your winks, and I'll take charge of Eunice at once."

"Well, thanks," said Fatty, relieved. "I must say she would rather cramp my style if she stuck to me like a leech all afternoon. And remember, not a word in front of Eunice about this business. If anyone is careless enough to drop a hint without meaning to, they'll have to retire from this mystery altogether."

This was a truly awful threat, and Bets felt quite scared. She decided that it would be best if she hardly spoke at all when Eunice was near. Fatty grinned at her serious face.

"It's all right, young Bets. You won't let us down. You never have yet. The one I'm really afraid of is Buster. He's been listening to us with pricked ears the whole time. Buster – don't you dare to give anything away to that girl, will you?"

"Wuff!" said the little Scottie, joyfully, sensing that the solemn meeting was at an end, and that Fatty was relaxing. He rolled over for his tummy to be tickled.

"Well – where do we meet?" asked Daisy. "Gosh, look, there's *Eunice*! She's tracked us down!"

"And she thinks I'm miles away running for all I'm worth!" said Fatty, horrified. "Quick – go out of the summer-house, all of you, and leave me here. Take the girl indoors and stuff her with biscuits, or something. She's always willing to eat."

Hurriedly the others went out of the little summer-house to meet a rather sulky Eunice. "Hallo!" she said. "Where's Fatty? His mother said he might be at Pip's, so I went there, and Pip's mother said you were all meeting here, so I came on here."

"Welcome!" said Larry, with a much-too-bright smile. "Come indoors and have a snack. I hope you like ginger-bread biscuits. Wherever can old Fatty be? I hope he won't wear himself out, running for miles and miles – *do* come in, Eunice! This way!"

A Little about Beetles

Fatty, left by himself in the summer-house with Buster, stayed there for some while, fearing that he might be seen by the sharp-eyed Eunice. But then, as the coast seemed quiet and clear, he stepped out briskly, made his way to the side gate and disappeared into the road.

Only Bets saw him go. She was watching the gate, knowing that he would probably slip out there when he thought it was safe. She went quickly out of the room, ran down the stairs and out into the garden. She tore after Fatty, shouting.

He turned, and when he saw it was only Bets, he stopped. "What is it?" he said, as she came running up out of breath. "Don't tell me Eunice saw me!"

"No, she didn't," panted Bets. "But we didn't arrange what time to meet this afternoon at the Fair, or where."

Fatty considered. "I should think three o'clock would be a good time," he said. "There will be heaps of people there then, and the man we're looking for would probably think it safe to be there. He may possibly have taken a job at the Fair, you know."

"Yes. So he might," said Bets. "Perhaps that's how it was that he has been seen here."

"You go back to the others," said Fatty, giving Bets a pat. "Don't say you've seen me, of course."

"What are you going to do?" asked Bets. "You aren't *really* going to go running, are you?"

"Yes. I am," said Fatty. "Somehow I've got to take off at least half my fat. So I and Buster will now race at a good speed round the county of Bucks. So long, young Bets!"

Bets watched him set off at a steady trot, with Buster at his heels. She hoped he wouldn't get too thin. He wouldn't be Fatty then, the Fatty she liked so much. She went back to the others, wondering if they had thought of any way of getting rid of the loud-voiced Eunice.

Fatty really did have a long run that morning. For one thing it was a lovely April day, and for another he quite enjoyed stretching his legs and running so steadily. He ran by the river mostly, and then turned when he got to Marlow, and went back again.

Jog-jog-jog, jog-jog-jog. Fatty's alert mind ran as steadily as his feet all the time he jogged along. Why had that escaped prisoner come to Peterswood? Had he friends there? Where was he sleeping at night? Was he dossing down behind some haystack or in somebody's garden? What work was he doing? He had to get money to keep himself, presumably, unless he had friends to help him. The Fair was certainly the likeliest place to look for him.

He came to Peterswood, turned up from the river into the road that led to the village, and jogged up it. He glanced at his watch. Yes – he had made good time. He turned the corner abruptly and was almost knocked down by a bicycle.

"Hey!" said Mr. Goon's familiar voice. "What you doing – you almost knocked me off my bike."

"Well, you nearly knocked *me* down!" said Fatty, jogging on without stopping. Goon swung his bicycle round and followed him, riding beside him, much to Fatty's annoyance.

"What's the idea?" asked the annoying Mr. Goon, pedalling along, keeping out of Buster's way – though by this time Buster was far too tired to snap at anyone's ankles, even Goon's.

"What's *what* idea?" said Fatty. "Haven't you ever seen anyone running before?"

"Yes. But what have you suddenly *started* it for?" asked Mr. Goon, wondering whether this outbreak of running had anything to do with hunting escaped prisoners.

"To slim down," said Fatty. "And it wouldn't be a bad thing if you did the same, Mr. Goon. Think how easy it would be to chase tramps and people like that if you were really in training, and could run fast!"

"You seen any more of that old tramp in your shed?" asked Mr. Goon.

"No. Have you?" said Fatty and ran to a stile, climbed over it and jumped down into the field. He was tired of Mr. Goon.

"There now – I wanted to find out if the Chief had gone and told him anything about that escaped prisoner," thought Goon. "I don't want that fat boy messing about looking for him, always turning up everywhere. Drat him!"

Eunice came home in time for lunch, having spent what she considered to be a very pleasant morning with the others. Fatty wondered if *they* had found it quite so pleasant! He himself had arrived back at twelve o'clock and had spent the rest of the morning in peace and quiet, down in his shed, looking through all his belongings there, in case a sudden disguise should be needed.

"We're all going to the Fair this afternoon," she announced to Fatty, as soon as he came into lunch, looking spick and span in grey flannels.

"Good," said Fatty, politely.

"But I warn you – don't try throwing any rings at the hoopla stalls," said Eunice.

"Why not?" asked Fatty, surprised.

"Well, because they're a fraud," said Eunice. "The rings are made just *too* small to fit over anything – anything decent that is, I mean – it's no good throwing for a clock, or anything like that – you'd never get it."

"Stuff," said Fatty, who considered himself very good at hoopla. "I've often won things at hoopla stalls. *You* probably don't win anything because you're not good at throwing."

Mr. and Mrs. Trotteville came in with Mr. Tolling. He beamed round through his thick glasses. "Well! And how have you two been getting on together this morning? I hope you've played together nicely."

"Father! DON'T talk as if we were seven years old!" said Eunice. "As a matter of fact, I've hardly *seen* Frederick this morning."

"Oh, Frederick – didn't you look after Eunice?" said his mother. "She's your guest, you know."

"I've been cross-country running," said Fatty. "Eunice was with the others. Mother – do I look any thinner?"

"Well, no," said his mother, looking at him carefully. "And I don't suppose you *will* look any thinner so long as you eat so many potatoes, Frederick. Look how many you've taken – five!"

"Gosh, so I have," said Fatty, quite startled. "And I only meant to take two." He put three back, looking rather gloomy.

"I'm much looking forward to my first Conference at your Town Hall tomorrow," said Mr. Tolling, taking quite a lot of potatoes himself. "Some very distinguished people will be there."

"Who?" asked Fatty, politely.

"Well, there will be William Wattling," said Mr. Tolling.

"He is *the* expert on the Cross-Veined Three-Spot Mackling Beetle of Peruvia. A wonderful man – truly wonderful. He spent one whole week lying outside this beetle's hole, in the middle of a swamp."

"Good heavens! I wonder he's alive to tell the tale!" said Mr. Trotteville, startled at this revelation of what a beetle-lover would do.

"And there's Maria Janizena," said Mr. Tolling, enjoying himself. "Now *she's* a marvel, she really is. Believe it or not, she found a batch of eighty-four eggs belonging to the Skulking Hunch-Beetle of Thibet, and hatched everyone out herself."

"What! Did she sit on them?" said Fatty, sounding amazed.

"Now, *Frederick*," said his mother. However Mr. Tolling apparently saw nothing but complimentary astonishment in Fatty's question, and went on solemnly.

"No, boy, no – of course not. She merely put the eggs in a warm cupboard – but the astonishing thing was, that when the eighty-four eggs hatched out, there were one hundred and sixty-eight young beetles – not eighty-four. Now what do you make of that strange fact?"

"All twins," said Fatty, solemnly, and was most gratified to hear Eunice give a loud guffaw and his father chuckle loudly.

"Shall we change the subject?" asked Mrs. Trotteville. "I keep thinking I see beetles in the cabbage."

"Really Mrs. Trotteville?" said Mr. Tolling, full of immediate interest. "Where? I must examine them."

Now it was Fatty's turn to roar, and poor Mr. Tolling looked bewildered.

"Father's no good at seeing a joke," Eunice informed the company. "Are you, Father?"

"Who else will be at the Conference?" asked Fatty. "Will they *all* be experts?"

"Most of them, my boy, most of them," said Mr. Tolling. "We would not welcome any novices at our meetings. I think I may say that every one of us there will have a large knowledge of the Coleoptera as a whole."

"And do *you* know everyone?" asked Fatty, thinking that if Mr. Tolling *did* know all these learned beetle-lovers, he could most certainly point out to Fatty anyone he did not recognize – and that might be a Most Suspicious Person – you never knew!

"No, my dear boy – I don't know all of them," said Mr. Tolling. "I have the list of all those who are going to attend the Meeting, here in my wallet – and I know perhaps half of them."

"Could I see the list sometime, sir?" asked Fatty, eagerly. If he went to the Meetings and saw someone like the escaped prisoner, he could check him on the list – and if he was not down on it, well, that would be very suspicious indeed!

"Yes, Frederick, certainly," said Mr. Tolling, most gratified to think that Fatty should show such interest. "I take it that you will like to come to one or more of the Meetings? I can vouch for you, of course, at the door. No strangers are allowed in, unless vouched for."

That was really interesting news. It looked as if any checking-up would be fairly easy. Fatty took the list of names from the obliging Mr. Tolling with warm thanks. "And I'll certainly be coming to some of the Meetings, sir," he said, much to the amazement of his parents. "The Coleoptera are most interesting – *most* interesting! Mother, do you remember those two stag-beetles I had when I was at kindergarten – the ones that kept fighting each other?"

Mr. Tolling looked pained, and Mrs. Trotteville frowned at Fatty. Really this was going too far. She couldn't understand why Fatty was playing up to the very boring Mr. Tolling in this way. Fatty saw her frown and changed the subject in his usual cheerful way.

"We're all going to the Fair this afternoon!" he said. "Mr. Tolling, you come too – it'll be a change from beetles. Come and ride on the roundabout."

"Well," said Mr. Tolling, most surprisingly, "I think I

will! It's years since I went to anything but meetings – yes, Frederick, I'll accept your kind invitation with pleasure!"

Whew! What a shock that was for Fatty!

Fun at the Fair

Larry, Daisy, Pip and Bets were extremely surprised when they saw Fatty coming to meet them at the Fair, accompanied by Mr. Tolling. It was bad enough to have Eunice – but here was her father too! Whatever could Fatty be thinking of?

"Sorry," said Fatty, when he got Larry to himself for a moment. "I just asked him to come for a joke – pulling his leg, you know – and he accepted! You could have knocked me down with a feather – or a beetle!"

"You really are an ass," said Larry, in disgust. "Now we've got to drag the two of them about with us. And did Mr. Tolling *have* to come to a Fair dressed like that – in town clothes, all muffled up as if it was a winter's day. He looks queer enough anyhow, with his beard and thick glasses. Honestly, we'll be laughed at wherever we go."

"I tell you, I'm sorry," said Fatty, annoyed. "How was *I* to know he'd say he'd come? Shut up about it and let's go round the Fair. And look out for You Know What."

The Fair was quite an ordinary one, with a roundabout, swings, hoopla stalls, a shooting-range, cake and sweet stalls, and various small side-shows. The little company walked round it, trying their luck at the hoopla, where Eunice proved most annoyingly right. Nobody's rings fell completely round anything.

"I told you so," she said, which impelled Fatty to waste another shilling trying to prove her wrong.

"There you are!" she said. "I *told* you the rings are too small. They always are!"

51

"Here, Miss – don't you say things like that!" said the boy in charge. "It's just that you ain't got the right knack of throwing, see? You watch *me* do it!"

And he climbed out of his stall, took a handful of rings and proceeded to throw each one round something – a packet of cigarettes, a clock, a vase and a box of chocolates. He grinned at Eunice's crestfallen face.

"Easy when you know how," he said. "Have another shilling's worth?" But nobody would!

Mr. Tolling appeared to enjoy himself extremely. He tried the hoopla. He bought sweets and even sucked them himself. He went on the little Dodgem motor-cars with Eunice, and put up bravely with her desire to bump violently every car in sight.

"Can't get rid of him," sighed Fatty to Daisy. "Have you seen anyone *interesting* – you know what I mean, don't you?"

"Yes. But I haven't," said Daisy. "Look. Let's go in here – where that clown is calling out something about boxing. If it's clowns boxing, it ought to be funny."

It wasn't. It was merely a boxing-ring into which anyone could step to box with a stalwart youngster called Champ Charlie. Daisy was not in the least interested in boxing and Fatty took her out again, laughing at the clown's antics as he did so. Then his face suddenly changed and he stared hard. Daisy wondered why, and she gazed at the clown too, with his painted face and white-gloved hands.

Fatty took Daisy off and they went behind a tent. "That clown!" said Fatty. "Did you see his painted face? There was a big red line all over the space between his mouth and nose – where the escaped prisoner is known to have a noticeable scar?"

"Oh, Fatty, yes!" said Daisy. "And his hands were gloved. They might be very knobbly for all we know."

"And his eyes were sharp, roving everywhere, did you notice?" said Fatty. "We can't see what kind of hair he's got because he had a clown's close-fitting cap on. He was

52

about medium height too. I say – I just wonder!"

"Well – he's our first Suspect," said Daisy. "We may find two or three more! Let's have one more look at the clown and then we'll go somewhere else. I don't know where the others are, but that doesn't matter. Come on."

They went to have a good look at the clown again. He was calling out in a raucous voice "Come on in, folks – see some fine boxing! Only sixpence a time, come on in. See Champ Charlie knock 'em all out. Sixpence a time!"

Yes – his thickly painted mouth would certainly hide any scar above it, and his eyes were as sharp as needles as they raked the crowd for possible customers. Fatty pulled Daisy over to the stall opposite, which sold cups of tea.

"Cup of char, mate?" said the man there, and Fatty nodded.

"It's all right. He means tea," said Fatty, seeing Daisy's mystified look. He spoke to the man who was pouring out the tea.

"I seem to have seen that clown over there somewhere else," he said. "What's his name, do you know?"

"I don't," said the man, handing the cup. "I never saw him before. He's just called Bert."

"Does he travel with the Fair?" asked Fatty.

"How do I know?" said the man, turning to another customer. "Ask him yourself."

Fatty didn't want to. He decided that it would be best to go to the Fair the next morning, when there would be fewer people, and try to get into conversation with the clown when he wasn't so busy. He might find him out of his clown-costume then, and without his paint.

"Come on, Daisy," he said, seeing that she didn't like her tea. "Pour it away. I only wanted to get it to make an excuse to ask the man about that clown."

"I know," said Daisy. "Look, let's go into the shooting-range and look round there."

They went in, passing an old woman sitting on a chair, who tried to sell them tickets, and watched some young men shooting at ping-pong balls that bobbed up and down on little jets of water. Daisy nudged Fatty and nodded towards a man who had just come in, and was taking over from the boy who had been handing out the rifles.

Fatty was startled. At first sight the man looked very like the photograph of the escaped prisoner – sharp eyes, dark brows, thick dark hair. He was burnt very brown, and looked a thoroughgoing man-of-the-Fair.

Fatty pushed Daisy outside. "It isn't the fellow we're looking for," he said, regretfully. "There's no scar above his mouth – at first I thought his sunburn might have been painted on to hide it – but it isn't."

"And his hands weren't knobbly," said Daisy. "I looked at them specially. They're smooth – almost like a woman's hands."

"Anyway – if he *was* the fellow we want, he wouldn't go about openly like that with no disguise," said Fatty. "It's just a fluke that he's like him. We can wash him out."

"Let's just look into the shooting-range *once* more," said Daisy. They went back to it, passing the old woman sitting on a chair outside. She called to them in a cracked voice. "Take a shot, young sir, take a shot!"

"No, thanks," said Fatty, and looked in at the shooting-tent again. No – the man there was definitely too young to be the escaped prisoner, and, as Daisy said, his hands were very smooth. Fatty knew from experience that while it was possible to alter and disguise a face very easily, it was exceedingly difficult to disguise hands.

"Spare a copper, young miss," said the cracked voice of the old woman. Daisy looked down and pitied the poor old creature. Her face was screwed-up and full of wrinkles, though her eyes were still lively. She had a filthy shawl pulled over her head, and her skinny bony hands clutched the roll of tickets.

Daisy nudged Fatty as they went by. "What a pity that man in there didn't have knobbly hands like that old woman!" she said. "We'd *really* have thought he might have been the man we want!"

"We shall get knobbly hands on the brain soon," said Fatty. "Let's go and find the others. But I say, look – DO look, Daisy!"

Daisy looked where Fatty nodded, and saw a fat red-faced man watching the swings. He had a red moustache and a little red beard. He wore no collar, but a dirty blue muffler instead, and a blue cap pulled right down over his forehead. His tweed coat was too tight for him, and his grey flannel trousers a little too short. Altogether he was a figure of fun, and passers-by laughed when they saw him.

"Do you know who that is?" said Fatty in a low voice to Daisy. She shook her head.

"Oh, Daisy, Daisy – you'll never make a detective!" said Fatty, disappointed. And then Daisy gave a little squeal and turned laughing eyes on Fatty.

"Sh!" said Fatty, warningly, and guided Daisy away to a distant corner, where she laughed loud and long.

"Oh, Fatty – it was *Mr. Goon* in disguise!" she giggled. "Oh, do let's find the others and see if they've spotted him. Oh dear – *why* does he make himself so very very conspicuous! Fancy trailing a Suspect in that get-up – he'd be noticed at once! Oh, that red moustache!"

They saw the others in the distance and ran to join them. As soon as they came near Larry called out. "Have you seen Goon? We nearly died of laughing!"

"Yes, we saw him," said Fatty. "What a sight! I say – do let's go and ask him the time, or something! We won't let on that we know him. He'll be so bucked to think we haven't seen through his disguise!"

"Yes – quick, come on while he's still over there!" said Pip. "I'll go up and ask him the time first – then you can go and ask him something, Bets – and then Larry. Quick!"

They wandered near Mr. Goon, who was now watching the Dodgem cars with much concentration, his cap almost hiding his eyes. Pip went up to him.

"Please, sir, could you tell me the time?" he said. Goon looked surprised when he saw that it was Pip, and then

55

"But I say, look – do look, Daisy!"

grunted. "Four o'clock or thereabouts," he said, putting on a very deep voice, which made Pip jump.

"Thank you, sir," said Pip, and went back to the others, chuckling.

Goon obviously felt pleased that his disguise was apparently so good. He even wandered nearer to where the children stood watching the roundabout. Ho, he thought, they didn't know it was he, Goon, who was there keeping a sharp eye on them! He walked past them, whistling. Bets ran after him.

"Oh, please," she said, "do you know what time the Fair closes?" Goon cleared his throat and put on his deep voice again.

"About half-past ten," he said, and then feeling his moustache coming loose, he put up his hand hurriedly to press it back. Bets gave a sudden giggle and fled.

Larry tried next. He walked close to Goon, pretended to pick something up from the ground and looked at it. Then he turned round. "Have you dropped this button, sir?" he asked. As it was one that Daisy had hurriedly twisted off her red dress, it obviously wasn't Goon's!

Goon cleared his throat again. "No, my boy, it is not mine," he said. "Er – are you enjoying yourself?"

"Oh, very much, sir, thank you!" said Larry – and then up came Fatty.

"Please, sir, I'd like to know where you got those policeman's boots you're wearing?" he said sternly. "I mean – I hope they're not stolen, sir."

"You toad of a boy!" said Goon, reverting to his own voice. "You *would* say a thing like that. Clear orf!"

"Good gracious – it's *you*, Mr. Goon!" gasped Fatty. looking quite flabbergasted. "Well now, who would have thought it!"

"I said – 'CLEAR ORF!'" thundered Mr. Goon, much to the surprise of everybody nearby. And Fatty "cleared orf", laughing till the tears came into his eyes. Poor old Goon!

"Where's Eunice?" said Fatty, when he and the others had finished laughing. "Has she gone home?"

"No. She wanted to go in a swing with her father, so we left her to it," said Larry. "Honestly, Mr. Tolling is a surprise! He's trying everything!"

"Where is he now?" asked Fatty.

"I expect they've gone to the roundabouts," said Daisy. "I heard Mr. Tolling say he'd like to. Goodness – he won't be fit to face the beetles tomorrow!"

"There they are, look," said Pip, as they strolled near the roundabout. It was going on its circular tour for the ten-thousandth time, churning out its old-fashioned tune.

"Not many people on it," said Fatty. "Only about seven or eight. What about us having a ride? Look – it's slowing down."

Everyone got off except for one person. That was Mr. Tolling. Eunice called to him. "It's stopped, Father!"

"I'm having another go," said the surprising Mr. Tolling. He was clutching the tall neck of a giraffe, and looked very peculiar, sitting on the big wooden creature in his dark town clothes.

"All right. But it makes me feel sick," said Eunice. "You go on alone. Oh – here are the others. Are you going on the roundabout, Frederick?"

"We thought we would," said Fatty, and paid for everyone. "Sure you won't, Eunice? Right! Get on, everybody! Choose some kind of animal to ride!"

Mr. Goon wandered over to the roundabout. He looked keenly at the roundabout boy, as if wondering if *he* might be a disguised prisoner. Then he looked sharply at a man going by wheeling a barrow.

"He's feeling very important, wearing a disguise and peering at everyone," said Larry to Daisy. "I can't say his disguise is a very good one. He looks *exactly* what he is – a policeman in disguise!"

They gazed at him, and then saw him give a slight start, as if he were surprised. He was looking at the roundabout, staring hard at Mr. Tolling.

"Why is he staring at Eunice's father?" wondered Daisy. She leaned over to where Fatty was riding an absurdly large duck that rose and fell as soon as the roundabout began. "Fatty – look at old Goon. He's staring at Mr. Tolling as if he's seen a ghost."

Fatty looked at Goon and then at Mr. Tolling. "Well – he's never seen Mr. Tolling in out-door clothes before," he said, "and honestly he looks a bit queer, doesn't he? Perhaps old Goon thinks he's the escaped prisoner!"

"Oh, *Fatty*! I believe he really *does* think that!" said Daisy, with a little squeal of laughter. "He can't take his eyes off him!"

Fatty gazed at Mr. Tolling again. He suddenly saw why Mr. Goon might possibly be thinking that Eunice's father was the man they were looking for! Yes – the right height – a moustache and beard – intelligent eyes – knobbly hands. Good gracious – he couldn't *be* that escaped prisoner, could he?

Fatty pulled himself together. "Don't be an ass!" he said to himself. "You know jolly well he's your father's friend and Eunice's parent. But gosh, I might have thought the same as Goon is thinking, if I didn't *know* who he was!"

The roundabout had now begun its usual journey, and the raucous music rang out all over the Fair. Every time that Mr. Tolling and his giraffe came round in front of Mr. Goon's eyes, the policeman stared and stared. Fatty began to laugh.

Now what would Goon do? Arrest poor Mr. Tolling? Oh no – that would never do. Eunice would be really shocked and upset.

The roundabout slowed down again, and at last stopped. Mr. Tolling was on the opposite side to Mr. Goon and got off there. He called to Eunice, who was nearby waiting for him.

"I'm going back now. I told Mrs. Trotteville I'd be in to tea, and I see it's late. You go back to your friends, Eunice."

Eunice went off at once to join the others, who were now all getting off the roundabout. Fatty looked for Mr. Goon, who was nowhere to be seen. And then he spotted him. Yes – there he was, trailing Mr. Tolling across the Fair towards the gate. Good gracious – so he really *did* think that Mr. Tolling was the escaped prisoner!

"I say!" said Fatty, pulling Larry and Daisy aside from Eunice and the others. "I say – I think old Goon has some-how got the idea that Mr. Tolling is the man we're after! I'll follow him to see what happens, and you two stay here with the others. Goon might notice *three* of us behind him – I'll see that he doesn't spot *me*! I may have to rescue Mr. Tolling from the clutches of the law!"

Daisy laughed. "All right – you follow them. I'll go back to the others, but we won't say a word to Eunice, or she'll be after you like a shot."

Fatty started off across the Fair field, and soon saw Goon not far in front of him. There wasn't much fear of the disguised policeman looking round and seeing Fatty, because he was obviously so intent on his own prey. Mr. Tolling was hurrying along – he must be hungry for his tea, thought Fatty!

And then Mr. Tolling unfortunately lost his way! He took the wrong turning, and went off towards Maidenhead instead of Peterswood. Fatty felt cross. Now they would go miles out of their way!

Mr. Tolling suddenly realized that he was on the wrong road and stopped. He looked up and down the street, hoping to see someone from whom he might ask the right way. He was short-sighted, and peered into the distance, delighted to make out someone at last. It was Mr. Goon, of course, sauntering up behind him.

"Oh, pardon me – but could you please put me on the right road to Peterswood?" said Mr. Tolling, politely. "I seem to have taken the wrong turning." He gazed up at Goon in surprise. What a peculiar-looking person!

Goon stared down at him most forbiddingly. Was that a scar under that moustache? "I'll take you back on the right road myself," said Goon. "We'll, er – have a little conversation on the way."

"Oh, you don't need to come *with* me," said Mr. Tolling, feeling quite alarmed at Goon's fierce gaze. "Just tell me the road to take."

"This way," said Goon, almost as if he were taking someone off to prison. He actually took firm hold of Mr. Tolling's arm. But Mr. Tolling shook it off angrily.

"If you behave like this I shall give you in charge for molesting me!" he said. "You must be one of those awful fellows from the Fair."

"Here – that's enough!" said Goon, annoyed. "All right – go by yourself if you want to! That's the way, see?"

Mr. Tolling went on by himself, turning round every now and again to see if Goon was following him. He was most annoyed to find that he was. Awful fellow with his silly red moustache and beard! Surely he didn't mean to rob him!

Goon kept quite close behind him, and Mr. Tolling hurried a little, trying to get rid of him. Goon hurried too. Fatty, who had kept well out of sight, grinned as he saw what was going on. Poor Mr. Tolling – he must be very fed up with Goon on his heels all the time. He decided to rescue him.

He came out from behind a bush with Buster as Mr. Tolling passed, and hailed him. "Hallo, sir! What are you doing here? We thought you'd gone home."

"Oh – Frederick – I'm *so* pleased to see you," said Mr. Tolling, delighted. "I took the wrong road. I asked that fellow behind there to tell me the way, and he was most unpleasant – most familiar too. I half thought he might be thinking of robbing me!"

"Don't worry about that," said Fatty, comfortingly, and, to Goon's amazement, he took hold of Mr. Tolling's arm. Goon, of course, still had no idea that it was Mr. Tolling in front of him, and he could not imagine why Fatty appeared to be so friendly with him. Then a very worrying thought crossed his mind. Of course! Fatty must have the same idea as he, Goon, had – he probably thought that that fellow might be the man they were both looking for! The Chief Inspector must have told Fatty about him when he went to see him about that tramp.

He followed them both, annoyed to see that Fatty was on apparently such friendly terms with the man. Was he questioning him – finding out all about him? Goon went a little closer, afraid that Fatty was finding out all that he, Goon, ought to know. Where were they going, anyhow? Would Fatty take the man right to where he was hiding, supposing that he *was* the escaped prisoner? That would be too good to be true – but Goon didn't want that. He didn't want Fatty interfering at all!

To his enormous surprise Fatty turned down the road that led to his own home! He and the man now appeared to be the best of friends. Goon hurried right up to them, and joined them. Mr. Tolling looked at him with dislike.

"What do you want, fellow?" he said. "Why are you trailing behind us like this? I shall give you in charge if you aren't careful!"

Fatty chuckled. Goon glared at him. "Where are you going?" he demanded.

"Home," said Fatty, looking mildly surprised. "Where are *you* going?"

"Who *is* this man?" said Mr. Tolling, puzzled and exasperated. "I'm tired of him."

"So am I," said Fatty, and took Mr. Tolling's arm again. "Come on – we're almost home."

Goon followed, frowning. Surely Fatty *wasn't* going to

take this fellow to his own home? Toad of a boy! Always leading him a dance!

Fatty came to the front gate of his house and held it open politely for Mr. Tolling, who went through thankfully. Goon stared, astounded. What *was* all this?

"You've a very short memory, Goon," said Fatty, as he closed the gate. "Don't you remember Mr. Tolling? You saw him yesterday, when you were called in about that fellow you thought was a tramp – the one down in my shed, you know. You didn't recognize *him* either, did you?"

Goon stared after Fatty as he and Mr. Tolling went up the drive to the front door, his head in a whirl. Good heavens, yes – of *course* that was the fellow he had seen with Mr. Trotteville yesterday – only he looked so different in his out-door clothes! And what did Fatty mean about that tramp? Why should he, Goon, have recognized that dirty old fellow?

It suddenly dawned upon poor old Goon that he should indeed have recognized the tramp! It must have been Fatty himself! And he had told the Chief Inspector a lot of nonsense about him – how strong and violent he had been – and how that dog Buster had bitten the tramp's ankles to the bone – and – and . . .

Goon gave a deep groan and went slowly to his own house. So *that* was why the Inspector had wanted to go and ask Fatty all about the tramp. *He* had guessed it was Fatty all the time. Another bad mark for Goon! "Pest of a boy!" muttered Goon to himself, as he let himself in at his front door. "He knows about that escaped prisoner too – and if I don't look out, he'll spot him before I do. That's what they were all at the Fair for!"

Poor Goon – he was so upset that he couldn't even eat his tea. That fat boy – if only he could get his hands on him!

Fatty has Trouble with Eunice

Fatty and Mr. Tolling were extremely late for tea, which had been cleared away. Mr. Tolling apologized profusely, and Jane brought in some fresh tea, complete with hot scones and chocolate cake.

Fatty was glad that he had brought Mr. Tolling home. Nobody would have *thought* of bringing Fatty tea if he had arrived when it had been cleared away – but now here was a perfectly splendid tea, all because of Mr. Tolling and his apologies.

Mr. Tolling described his adventures at the Fair, and then how he had been followed home by what he called "a half-mad, very nasty-looking fellow with no manners at all." Fatty grinned. He wished that Goon could have heard that!

Eunice arrived much later, having been given tea by Larry at the Fair. She was cross that Fatty had gone off home without her.

"Well, I saw your father in difficulties," said Fatty. "And I felt I *must* see him home. He had lost his way."

"Well, really, Father," said Eunice. "You'll lose yourself on your way to bed one of these days!"

"Hadn't you and Eunice better have a nice game of chess?" said Mrs. Trotteville, to Fatty's horror. Before he could think of an excuse to say no, Eunice had arranged everything in her maddeningly competent way, getting the chessboard out and setting out the men.

"Ha – two school champions," said Mr. Trotteville, with interest, and put down his paper to watch. But he soon became bored, for Eunice took at least twenty minutes before she made a move. Fatty was a much quicker player, and he soon grew bored too, and began going over all the happenings at the Fair in his mind.

"That clown," he thought, "we must certainly find out about him. And that boy in the shooting-range who was so like the photo of the escaped man. Does *he* come into the picture anywhere? I can't see how. Well, tomorrow morning I'll go to the Fair again and talk to that clown – and in the afternoon I'll go along to the Coleopterist Meeting, and just have a good look round there."

"Your turn, Frederick," said Eunice, impatiently. "You're not paying attention."

Fatty made his move at once, and Eunice again fell into a kind of trance, gazing at the chessmen intently. Poor Fatty became more and more bored. Chess was always a slow game – but this was dreadful!

Mr. Tolling began talking about the Fair again, and how he had enjoyed it. "There was only one thing I forgot to go and see," he said. "And that was the Flea-Circus. How anyone can ever be fond enough of insects to train fleas to perform tricks I simply do not know!"

"Good gracious! I'd rather walk ten miles than go near a flea-circus!" said Fatty's mother, horrified. "Are fleas really clever enough to be trained, Mr. Tolling? And do people ever train beetles?"

"Fleas are highly intelligent," said Mr. Tolling. "Beetles vary. Now the *most* intelligent beetle known is found in the Atlas Mountains at a height of two thousand feet. It actually sews leaves together to . . ."

But why the beetle sewed leaves together Fatty didn't hear, because an idea had suddenly flashed into his mind.

"A *flea*-circus!" he thought. "Of course – the fellow we're after is keen on insects. *He might be looking after the fleas!* Gosh, I never even knew there was a flea-circus at the Fair! I must certainly go to it tomorrow, and have a look. I wonder if the others knew about it. As soon as I've made my next move, I'll go and telephone Larry."

Eunice at last made a move, and Fatty at once made his. Eunice frowned. "You ought to think longer," she said. "No good chess-player plays quickly."

"I have plenty of time to think out my moves while

you're thinking out yours," said Fatty. "That's more than enough time, my dear Eunice. As for trying to tell me I'm not a good player, you just wait till you're well and truly whacked – then you'll know who's the good player! Excuse me a moment – I have to go and telephone."

Eunice was not pleased. She bent her head over the chess-board again, determined to beat Fatty. He went out into the hall and looked round and about cautiously. Nobody appeared to be within listening-range.

He was soon speaking to Larry. "I say, Larry, thanks for giving Eunice tea. I had a funny time going after Mr. Tolling. Listen. I can't talk loudly, so glue your ear to the receiver."

He told Larry how Goon had followed poor Mr. Tolling and scared him, and how puzzled and exasperated Goon had been when he, Fatty, had taken Mr. Tolling right in at his front gate. Larry roared.

"You always get the exciting bits, Fatty," he said. "What about tomorrow? Do we all meet at the Fair again – to see that clown?"

"Yes – and I say – did you know there was a flea-circus there?" asked Fatty. "I didn't."

"Oh yes – I saw a notice up," said Larry. "But gosh, Fatty – you don't want to go to a *flea*-circus, surely! Why, even Buster hates fleas."

"Larry – think back to those notes about You-Know-Who!" said Fatty, lowering his voice. "Remember what he liked?"

"Yes. Cats," said Larry. "There wasn't anything about liking fleas though. I'm sure there wasn't."

"I know – but there was a bit about being interested in *insects*," said Fatty.

"Oh my goodness, yes!" said Larry. "Of course. I just thought of butterflies or moths or beetles or bees – not of fleas. Well, we'd better visit the flea-circus tomorrow then. There may be a clue there."

"Yes. Meet at the cross-roads by the bus-stop at ten o'clock," said Fatty. "Tell Pip and Bets, will you? I must get back to my game of chess. At the rate we're playing it I probably shan't be able to meet you at ten tomorrow! Goodbye."

He put down the receiver and went back to the chess-board. Eunice had just made a move. To Fatty's horror he saw that it was an extremely good move – a master-move, in fact – and that if he didn't think really hard he might find himself check-mated.

So for the next ten minutes he forgot all about clowns and flea-circuses and fairs, and frowned over the chess-men. However, he need not have worried, because in the end Buster brought the game to a very sudden finish.

The Scottie had been lying quietly under the little chess-table when he thought he heard the scratch-scratch-scratch of a mouse in the wainscoting nearby. He pricked up both ears, and turned his head towards the noise. To his joy the mouse actually came out of a small hole and ran across the room.

Buster leapt up in excitement and upset the chess-table! All the pieces were scattered on the floor, and Eunice shouted in exasperation. "What did he want to do that for? Just as I had got you into a hole, too, Frederick. Two more moves and I would have check-mated you!"

"You wouldn't," said Fatty. "Buster, stop barking, you ass. You'll bring Mother in here."

"I shall put all the pieces back again on the board," said Eunice, firmly. "I remember where they were – and we'll go on playing."

Fatty groaned. He had never been so tired of a game of chess before.

"What made Buster upset the table like that?" said Eunice, severely, picking up the pieces.

"Didn't you see the mouse run across the room?" asked Fatty. "It ran right by your chair. Buster saw it and . . ."

"What? A *mouse*?" said Eunice, with a shriek. "Oh *no*! I can't *bear* mice. Is it still here?"

"Bound to be," said Fatty, pleased to see that the bold, confident Eunice was trembling all over. Well, well – who would have thought it! Not even little Bets was afraid of mice! "It was a pretty big mouse, too – look, Buster is sniffing round your chair again."

Eunice gave another shriek and disappeared out of the door at sixty miles an hour. Fatty heaved a sigh of relief and immediately put the chessmen away in their box, then hid them at the back of his mother's sewing cupboard.

"And there they can stay till Eunice has gone," he decided. "Don't catch that mouse, Buster. It just about saved my life!"

The evening passed unexpectedly peacefully after that, because after supper had been cleared away Mr. Tolling announced that it would be nice to have a game of bridge.

"Eunice plays a wonderful game," he said to Mrs. Trotteville. "She and I will take you and your husband on, Mrs. Trotteville. I am sure that Frederick will not mind being left out."

Fatty was only too pleased! He wanted to think over the next morning's plans. He had almost decided that he would go to the Fair in some kind of disguise. It would be easier to mix with the fair-people then, and ask a few questions, and keep his eyes and ears open. He slipped down to his shed as soon as the four others were sitting quietly over the bridge table, Eunice, as usual, laying down the law to everyone.

He locked himself into his shed, drew the old curtains over the windows, and lighted his oil-lamp. Now – what about tomorrow's disguise?

"I'll go dressed as a youth who wants a job with the Fair," he thought. "I'll put a lot of sunburn colouring on my face – and I'll wear my false teeth over my own teeth in front – yes, and I'll walk with a bit of a limp. I bet none of the fair-people will think I'm anything to do with the party of children who visited the Fair only this afternoon!"

He spent a pleasant hour sorting out the clothes he meant to wear – a very disreputable pair of flannel trousers, with stains all down the legs – a coat that had once belonged to a gardener, and which Fatty had bought from him for two shillings – a pair of broken-down old shoes, bright yellow socks, and an extremely dirty shirt, striped in what once had been bright colours.

"Yes," said Fatty, looking at them. "You'll do fine! I'd better rub dirt into my finger-nails too. I forgot that once, and it gave me away! And where's that dirty old handkerchief? I'll put that into the coat-pocket."

He decided to get his mother on his side the next morning, so that she could give Eunice some job to keep her busy. Fatty felt that he really couldn't cope with Eunice any more. It would be too difficult to slip down to his shed and disguise himself if she was about.

So he took Mrs. Trotteville into his confidence that night. "Mother – *do* you think you could give Eunice a job to do for you tomorrow morning?" he asked. "I'm doing something special with the others, and it's not really fair on them to drag her about with us *all* the time. They were awfully good to her yesterday."

Mrs. Trotteville sympathized with Fatty just then, because she had become very tired of Eunice at the bridge table that evening. Eunice had had remarkably good cards, and had won every game. She had then proceeded to give the others a most competent lecture on how the game of bridge *ought* to be played, and Mrs. Trotteville had suddenly longed to slap her.

So she could quite see Fatty's point about keeping her busy the next day. "Yes, of course, Frederick," she said. "I'll ask her if she will take round the Parish magazines for me – I'm sure she will be thrilled to go round the village with them and tell everyone how to keep their gardens tidy or how to train their dogs!"

Fatty laughed and gave his mother a hug. "Thanks!" he said. "All the same, I wouldn't put it past Eunice to deliver all the magazines at top speed, and then come racing after us to see what *we're* doing!"

"You'd better put a mouse into your pocket," said his mother, much to Fatty's amusement. "You'd be *quite* safe then!"

Fatty and Bert the Clown

Fatty really enjoyed himself next morning down in his shed. He waited until Eunice had started off with the bundle of Parish magazines and then he began his disguising, whistling quietly to himself.

He gave himself a very brown face indeed. "As brown as the boy in the shooting-range!" he said. He then stuck on some shaggy eyebrows over his own, which gave him rather a forbidding expression. He ruffled his hair so that most of it stood up on end.

He dug his fingers into some dark earth just outside the shed and got his nails extremely dirty, and his hands too. Then he dressed himself in the old clothes, and finally put in the prominent false teeth. He looked in the glass and grinned, half startled himself to see the big teeth that stuck out over his lower lips.

"You'll do," he said. "What's your name, now? Bert? Sid? Alf? Yes, Alf, I think. Come on, Alf, it's time you went to make your enquiries at the Fair."

He slipped out of the shed, went to the little gate that led into the lane at the bottom of the garden and looked out. No one was about. He could go in safety.

He put his hands in his pocket and slouched down the road, whistling as best he could through his prominent front teeth. He had had to leave Buster behind, for Buster following at his heels would certainly give him away!

He had one very bad moment when he passed the gate of a house not far from his own. Someone came hurrying out and bumped into him. Fatty was about to raise his cap and apologize when he remembered that he was Alf. And then, to his horror, he saw that it was Eunice who had bumped into him. Some of her magazines had fallen to the ground.

"Well, you might at least say you're sorry, young man!" she said. "And can't you pick those up for me?"

"Pick 'em up yourself," mumbled Fatty, and ambled off, grinning at the look on Eunice's face. She hadn't had the slightest idea who he was. His disguise must be quite perfect!

Eunice stared after the slouching youth in disgust. "Dirty, ill-mannered lout," she said, and picked up her magazines. "I'd like to box his ears!"

Fatty made his way to the cross-roads, where he had planned to meet the others. Ah, yes – there they were, waiting. Good. They were looking down the road for him, but not one of them recognized him as he came shambling up, hands in pockets. He went right past them, grinning to himself.

He sat down on the bus-stop seat. "Got the time, Mister?" he called to Larry.

"Almost ten," said Larry.

There was a pause, and the others began to talk among themselves. "I hope he's got rid of Eunice," he heard Larry say. He called out to him again.

"Got a fag, Mister?"

"No," said Larry, shortly.

"When's the next bus?" asked Fatty. " 'Arf-past ten, ain't it?"

"There's a time-table there," said Pip, pointing to one. They all looked at the youth in disgust. Goodness, what a lout!

"He probably belongs to the Fair," said Daisy, and that made Fatty chuckle to himself. Then he heard the bus rumbling round the corner and stood up. The others gave a despairing look down the road. "Fatty's missed the bus," said Bets dolefully. "What do we do? Wait for the next one and see if he turns up?"

"No need to do that," said Fatty amiably, in his own voice. "We'll all catch this one. Come on!"

71

"When's the next bus?" asked Fatty

He roared at their amazed faces. They were so astonished that they almost missed the bus, for they stood rooted to the ground! Fatty had to hustle them in.

"Say nothing," he hissed. "Don't speak to me in the bus. I'll find some way of talking to you at the Fair."

The other four sat silent in the bus, quite overcome by Fatty's surprising appearance. Bets shot sidelong glances at him. Never, never would she have thought that it was Fatty sitting alongside her. *Was* it? Well, it must be, because of his voice. How clever he was!

They all got off at the Fair and went in at the gate. "You can follow me around," said Fatty, in a low voice. "Keep your eyes and ears open. I'm going to find the clown first."

He went on in front of them, and they followed. He came to the little boxing-tent and looked for the clown, but there was no one there. The tent was empty, except for the little boxing-ring.

"Who are you looking for, mate?" said a boy, passing by, carrying a bucket of water.

"Bert," said Fatty, remembering the clown's name. "The clown, you know."

"He's gone to have a tooth out," said the boy. "He'll be back in a few minutes. He was half-mad with toothache in the night."

"Right. I'll wait," said Fatty, and sat down on the grass. The other four heard all this, and wandered off, keeping a watch in case Bert came back.

Nobody recognized Bert when he did come back for he was not in his clown-suit. He had a shock of thick dark hair, and the whole of his face, except his sharp eyes, was covered by a dirty scarf. He came to the boxing-tent and was just about to go inside when Fatty spoke to him.

"Hey? You Bert the clown?"

"Yep," said Bert, from behind his scarf. "What's biting you, chum? You waiting for me?"

"Yep," answered Fatty. "I . . ."

"Oh -- then you'd be the boy old Dicky said he'd send along to help me," said Bert.

73

"Yep," said Fatty, thankfully. This was a bit of luck! "What do I have to do?"

"You good at figures?" asked Bert, his face still hidden by his scarf. "Here – I'll show you what kind of figures you'd have to keep. I'm no good at head-work, I'm not."

He disappeared into the tent and came out with a small account book which apparently showed the takings for each day. Fatty glanced at the hand that held it out to him. *What* a knobbly one! All bones. A little feeling of excitement crept up his spine.

"If only I could see his face now he hasn't got on any paint, I'd know then about the scar," thought Fatty, pretending to go through the account book. "His hair's right – and his eyes and eyebrows – and his height. How can I get him to take off that scarf?"

He handed back the book. "Reckon I could keep them figures for you okay," he said.

"When could you start, chum?" asked Bert.

"Tell you later on," said Fatty. "I got to go and see a bloke about another job first. That do?"

"Okay by me," said Bert. "Long as you let me know to-day." He was about to go into the boxing-tent when Fatty spoke to him again.

"What you done to your face?" he said. "Got a cold or something?"

"No," said Bert. "Had a tooth out, that's all, and the dentist said I'd better keep my face covered up with this cold wind about."

"Was it a bad tooth?" said Fatty, with much sympathy in his voice.

"Pretty bad," said Bert. "Right in the front too. Good thing I haven't got teeth that stick out like yours, or the gap would show like anything!"

"Let's see it," said Fatty. "I bet it won't notice much."

Bert promptly pulled down his scarf and opened his mouth. He pointed to a gap in his top teeth. "See? That's where he took it out. Had a root as long as a tree's!"

But Fatty was not looking at the teeth – he was looking

74

for a thin, curving scar just above the mouth! He stared hard.

There was no scar there! Not even the sign of where one might have been! Fatty was bitterly disappointed, for he really had thought that the clown was the man he wanted.

"Nasty place," he said. "I reckon it will soon heal though. "Well – so long!"

He could see the four others nearby, all gazing as hard as they could when the clown pulled off his scarf. He walked by them. "No go," he said out of the side of his mouth. "He's not the man. Everything fitted except the scar!"

"Let's go to the flea-circus now," said Larry to the others in a loud voice, meant to reach Fatty's ears. And off they all walked, passing Fatty on the way. They went in the direction pointed out by a wooden hand that had "Flea-Circus" painted on it.

But the flea-circus was not yet open. A flag flew at the top of a fairly big tent, with "Fangio's Famous Fleas" printed across it. Fatty peeped inside.

There was only an old woman there – the same old woman who had been sitting in a chair outside the shooting-tent the day before. She was over by a table that held big glass cages, gazing intently into them.

" 'Afternoon, Ma," said Fatty, and the old lady jumped at the sound of his voice. She turned her wrinkled face to him, pulling her dirty shawl over her head. "Is the flea-circus open, Ma?" asked Fatty. "There's some kids here want to see it."

"My daughter ain't here yet," said the old woman, in her cracked voice.

"Oh – does *she* run the flea-circus?" asked Fatty. "Who's Fangio then?"

"He was her father," said the old woman. "Dead now, though, so she runs it herself, Lucita does. Wunnerful creatures, them fleas. You can make 'em do anything you want to. And strong! Why, you should see what a load they can pull in this little cart!"

"Pull a *cart*! Surely fleas can't pull a *cart*!" said Larry, coming right into the tent. "Can we see the cart?"

"Yes, you come in," said the old woman, her face wrinkled up into what Larry supposed was meant to be a smile. *How* wrinkled she was – he wondered if she was a hundred years old! The untidy hair sticking out from under her shawl was white – a dirty white, it is true – but it would have been snowy-white if it had been clean.

"Are you Mrs. Fangio?" asked Daisy.

"That's right," said the old woman. "Come to help my daughter and my son at the Fair. My son's over at the shooting-tent."

Fatty remembered the son. So did they all! He had been so very like the photos of the escaped prisoner – except that he had no scar above his mouth, and his hands were not knobbly or bony.

"You see here now," said the old woman, eagerly. "Here's the little cart – and here's a crane the fleas work – and they can roll this little barrel along."

"How amazing!" said Daisy. "But where are the fleas? I hate fleas but I must say I'd like to have a look at such miraculous ones!"

"I'll show you!" said the old woman – but before she could even undo the tiny cages where the fleas were kept, an angry voice called loudly:

"Didn't I say you weren't to touch them fleas? You just keep your hands off them!"

Fatty Asks a Question

Everyone turned round at once. A girl stood in the doorway, a dark-haired, sharp-eyed, gypsy-looking young woman. Her thin mouth looked sulky as she stared at the little company.

76

"Now where have I seen her before?" thought Fatty at once. "She reminds me of someone. Where *have* I seen someone like her?"

The girl came into the tent, scowling. "Clear out," she said to the children, and then turned to Fatty, evidently regarding him as belonging to the Fair. "Clear those kids out. We don't allow anyone in the tent when there's no show on. Them fleas are valuable."

She then turned on the old woman. "Didn't you say you'd keep your hands off of them fleas?" she said. "Interfering again, I suppose! You let them be, they're mine."

"You shouldn't ought to talk to your old mother like that," said the old woman, darting a fierce glance at the young woman. She opened her mouth as if to make a sharp retort, looked at the children standing near the doorway, and thought better of it.

"Want any help here?" said Fatty, still wondering who it was that the girl reminded him of.

"Well, *she's* supposed to keep the tent clean," said the girl, with an angry look at the old woman. "But you can sweep it out if you want. I'll give you a shilling."

"But are you sure your mother won't mind?" said Fatty. "I don't want to do her out of a job."

"I've got another job tomorrow," cackled the old woman. "You can have this job, young feller – and I hope you don't feel the edge of that girl's tongue as often as I do! Fleas! I could manage fleas better than she can, before she was born."

"Oh, get out," said the young woman. "And don't go near Josef. He's in a vile temper today."

"What an unpleasant family!" thought Fatty, taking a broom from the back of the tent and beginning to sweep the littered ground. "Who's Josef?" he asked.

"My brother. Over at the shooting-tent," said the girl. "He's my twin."

Fatty stopped sweeping and looked at her. Of *course*! That was whom she reminded him of – the young man over at the shooting-tent, the one who was so like the

77

escaped prisoner. The same sharp eyes, dark brows, the same springing dark hair, thin mouth and sulky look. So they were twins – that explained the likeness!

"Got any more brothers or sisters?" he asked, wondering if perhaps there was another brother who might be the man he wanted.

"No. Josef and I are all that's left of our family," said the girl.

"And your mother," said Fatty, sweeping hard.

"Oh her – yes," said the girl, who obviously had no love for the old woman.

"Do you sleep here in this tent?" asked Fatty. He could not see any bedding and he wondered what the girl and her brother did at night.

"No! We have a caravan, down in Barker's Field," said the girl. "There's a crowd of them there. Want to know a lot, don't you? You new to the Fair?"

"Yes," said Fatty, truthfully. "Always had a liking for Fairs, so I came here to look for a job. I wouldn't mind working in a circus, either – especially with animals."

"Well, keep off lions and tigers," said the girl. "They'll flash out their paws at you for nothing when you pass them – and maybe scar you for life!"

"Talking of scars," said Fatty, "did you ever meet anyone with a scar curving above his upper lip?"

"And what do you mean by *that*?" said the girl, and she gave Fatty such a glare that he was astonished. "Go on – what do you mean by *that*?"

"Nothing," said Fatty, surprised.

"You clear out," said the girl, and held out a shilling. "And don't come back here."

"But why – what have I said to upset you?" asked Fatty. "I didn't mean . . ."

"Clear out or I'll have Josef run you out," said the girl, crisply, and Fatty decided that it was best to go, and go quickly. He went out of the tent, looked round for the others, and gave them a brief nod. Then he made for the gate, and went out. He waited outside for the four to come along.

"I do wish we could have seen those performing fleas," said Bets, as she came up. "Hallo, Fa . . ."

"Sh!" hissed Fatty, and Bets went red, remembering that Fatty must never be recognized when in disguise.

"We'll catch the bus back," said Larry, and they all made for the bus-stop, Fatty a little way behind, as if he did not belong to them.

The top of the bus was empty when they got on, so they all trooped upstairs. "Anything interesting, Fatty?" asked Larry.

"I don't know. I *think* so," said Fatty. "We won't talk here. All come down to my shed, please; we'll meet there. I want to talk something over."

Fatty leapt off the bus as soon as it stopped and made his way to the lane at the back of his garden. He slipped in through the little gate there and went cautiously to the nearby shed. Was Eunice anywhere about? She didn't appear to be. Good!

The others soon joined him, and he locked the door. "What's up, Fatty?" asked Larry. "Oh, blow – there's Buster outside – he must have heard our voices. I'll let him in."

Having let in the excited little Scottie, they all settled down again, and looked expectantly at Fatty.

"It's something that girl said – the girl that owns the fleas," said Fatty. "First of all, I must tell you that she's twin to that fellow in the shooting-tent – the one we thought was so like the escaped prisoner."

"Oh, I *thought* she reminded me of someone," said Bets. "Of course – that's who it was. Go on, Fatty."

"Well – I was sweeping out the tent for her, and talking," said Fatty, "and I happened to say that I'd like to work with animals, in a circus – and she said, 'Well, keep off lions and tigers. They'll flash out their paws at you for nothing when you pass them, and maybe scar you for life.' And *I* said, quite casually. 'Talking of scars, did you ever meet anyone with a scar curving above his upper lip?' "

"And what did she say then?" asked Pip.

"She said, 'And what do you mean by *that*?' " said Fatty, "and gave me such a glare. Then she said, 'You clear out and don't come back here.' Just like that."

There was a silence. "What did she mean?" said Daisy, puzzled.

"That's what *I* want to know," said Fatty. "My question disturbed her – maybe even frightened her. Why?"

"Because she jolly well *does* know someone with a scar above his upper lip!" said Larry. "That's why!"

"Exactly," said Fatty. "Now you see why I wanted to have a talk about it."

"My word – yes – we've got to get to the bottom of this," said Larry, excited. "If she does know someone with a scar like that, it's obviously the escaped prisoner. Well, he's not at the Fair. We've pretty well seen everyone closely now – so where is he?"

"Where does that girl live?" asked Pip. "In the Fair?"

"No – in a caravan that stands with a good many others in Barker's Field," said Fatty.

"Would she be hiding this fellow, do you think?" asked Larry. "In her caravan, perhaps? Would he be another brother?"

"No. She told me that she and her twin are all that's left of her family," said Fatty. "Except that ugly old mother, of course. But yet, she and her brother are so like the photo of that man, aren't they? I wonder if the Chief Inspector knows if there's another brother?"

"You could easily find out," said Pip. "Wait – doesn't it say in those notes you had?"

Fatty took them out of a drawer and the five of them examined them. "Yes – it says here – 'Family. No brothers or sisters. Father and mother dead. One uncle, dead. No children.' "

"Well – that girl and her twin *can't* be his brother or sister," said Larry. "All the same, Fatty, I wish you could have a snoop round their caravans!"

"So do I," said Fatty. "But I don't see how I can. I mean

– it stands among a lot of others, and I'd easily be seen prying round in the daytime – and at night they'd be in the caravan, and I wouldn't *dare* to go knocking at it!"

A voice broke into their conference. It was Eunice's! "Frederick! Are you in your shed? Don't you know it's lunch-time, and if you want to go to the first meeting this afternoon, you oughtn't to be late."

"Oh, blow Eunice!" said Fatty, in disgust. "Is it as late as that? Gosh, yes it is! Well, we seem to be up against a blank wall. Think about it, will you, and telephone me if anyone sees a way out! ALL RIGHT, EUNICE, I'M COMING!"

The others slipped quickly out of the shed, avoided Eunice, and went out of the little gate that led into the back lane. Fatty stripped off his filthy things, cleaned his face and dressed himself. He arrived five minutes late for lunch and sat down, apologizing.

"Sorry. Didn't notice the time!" he said. "Yes, I'll have some ham, please, Mother."

He took up his knife and fork, and then discovered that he had forgotten to clean his nails. They were still full of dirt he had forced into them! He tried to hold his knife and fork with bent fingers, so that his nails did not show. His mother noticed at once.

"Frederick! What's the matter, dear? Have you hurt your hands?"

Everyone immediately looked at Fatty's curiously bent fingers.

"Oh, it's nothing," said Fatty. "Just a touch of cramp, that's all."

Eunice at once took hold of his right hand and straightened the fingers as if to get the cramp out. "The best thing is to ..." she began, as Fatty snatched his hand away. But his mother had already seen the filthy nails and looked coldly at Fatty.

"Please go and do your nails, Frederick," she said, and Fatty fled, conscious of the shocked eyes of Mr. Tolling, his mother and Eunice. Thank goodness his father had gone back to his work!

"We shall be late, we shall be late," fussed Mr. Tolling, when Fatty came back and lunch proceeded on its leisurely way. "Frederick, are you sure you can be ready when Eunice is? Have you your ticket? We really must start soon. I do hope you will have a most enjoyable afternoon!"

Fatty was certain he wouldn't. He was sure that he would not find the escaped prisoner at the Coleopterist Conference. No – he would much more likely be found in a caravan in Barker's Field. What a *nuisance* to have to go to such a dull meeting – and with Eunice, of all people!

A Very Interesting Afternoon

It was only about seven minutes' walk to the Town Hall. Mr. Tolling hurried along, with Eunice and Fatty just behind. Quite a number of other people were hurrying along to the Town Hall too! Fatty was surprised to think that there were so many beetle-lovers staying in Peterswood.

He was also surprised to see how many of the men wore moustaches and beards. "Is it a sort of uniform with coleopterists to wear hair on their faces?" he enquired of Eunice.

"Don't be silly," she said. "Look, there's the wonderful Maria Janizena, the one who hatched out all those eighty-four beetles from Thibet."

"Oh yes, the one hundred and sixty-eight twins," said Fatty, remembering. He stared at the great Maria Janizena and shuddered. "She looks very like a big beetle herself," he said in a low voice to Eunice. "And those things sticking up in her hat are rather like the horns my stag-beetles had."

He expected Eunice to be angry and scornful at such a disrespectful remark, but to his surprise she gave a sudden giggle. "Don't," she said. "Father will hear."

They went up the steps of the Town Hall just behind

Mr. Tolling. When he was almost at the top Fatty had a shock. Mr. Goon was there, standing beside a man who held a long list in his hand, apparently helping with the checking of the members.

"Goon must have got some idea that the man we want will come here," thought Fatty, at once. "Now who told him that? The Chief Inspector? Or has he worked it out himself as I did – that the man is interested in insects, and so will come to the Conference – and may probably even be a member!"

Mr. Goon was even more surprised to see Fatty than Fatty was to see him. He scowled, and then looked quickly down the list held by the man standing near him. Mr. Tolling presented his ticket, and Eunice presented hers. Mr. Goon then barred Fatty's way.

"Sorry," he said. "Only ticket-holders admitted."

"Oh – *I'm* vouching for him. He's my guest for this Conference," said Mr. Tolling, much to Goon's annoyance. He let Fatty past, glaring at him. That boy! Always turning up where he wasn't wanted. Did *he* think too that that escaped prisoner might be somewhere about in this peculiar Conference?

Fatty sat down with Eunice and Mr. Tolling. He began to study the people around him. They all looked extremely earnest, almost as if they had come to church. The few women looked even more serious than the men. The wonderful Maria Janizena was up on the platform with the other big noises, the spiky things in her hat nodding to and fro as she spoke to the men on each side of her.

"Aren't there any beetles to see?" asked Fatty. "Is it going to be talky-talk all the time?"

"There's a show of beetles in another room, I think," whispered back Eunice. "There usually is. Very, very precious too they are – lots of them from different Collections! We'll go and see them afterwards. I'll show you some that my father caught. Very rare ones."

Fatty came to the conclusion that beetle-lovers were very much alike to look at – they were either bald and bearded, or bushy-haired and bearded. The few who had no moustache or beard stood out among the crowd, and it was only a minute's work to discover that not one had a curving scar above his upper lip.

"Not that I really had a hope to see one," thought Fatty. "Gosh, I wish I'd thought of disguising myself and painting a scar above my mouth, and coming here. Goon would have been too thrilled for words!"

He ran down the list of names of members obligingly lent to him by Eunice. Some of them were foreign and very queer-sounding – no help to Fatty at all. He began to feel that it was an utter waste of time to come to the meeting. The only thing that would be any real help would be to pull at a few moustaches and see if they came off and were hiding any scar beneath! But that unfortunately was impossible.

The meeting was even duller than Fatty had feared it might be, though Mr. Tolling appeared to enjoy it very much, listening intently to every word that was said by the speakers on the platform. Fatty began to yawn, though he tried his hardest to stop. Mr. Tolling gave him a stern look, but somehow that made Fatty yawn all the more.

He looked round to see if Mr. Goon was still at his place by the door. Yes, he was – presumably to stop any gate-crashers. As Fatty looked at him he yawned – a most prodigious yawn that set Fatty off again. He caught Fatty's eye and glared. Pest of a boy – copying his yawn like that! Goon spent a pleasant few minutes thinking of some of the things he would like to say to Fatty if only he had the chance.

At last, when Fatty was almost asleep, the meeting was over. "Now we go to the other room to examine the specimens," whispered Eunice. "They're really interesting. I'll show you Father's."

Goon was already in the outer room when the members filed in. Round the room were trestle-tables and on them were big cases, glass-fronted, in which were specimens of many different kinds of beetles.

"Are there any *live* beetles?" Fatty asked Mr. Tolling, who, with gleaming eyes, was already examining a case of curious horned beetles.

"Oh yes – there should be," said Mr. Tolling. He spoke to someone beside him, a man whom Fatty had seen sitting on the platform. "Good-afternoon, Sir Victor – may I congratulate you on your speech? And do you happen to know if there are any cases of live beetles – my young friend here wants to know."

"Oh yes, yes," said Sir Victor, whose beard reached almost down to the bottom of his waistcoat. "But we had a sad accident yesterday, when we were arranging them – two cases were carelessly handled, fell, and broke. Mercifully, most mercifully, we were able to capture all the live beetles but one."

"Aren't you showing those beetles then?" asked Mr. Tolling, disappointed.

"Yes. It so happened that the old woman engaged to come as a cleaner this week has a daughter who runs what is, I believe, called a flea-circus at some local fair – and as these people have well-made display cages for their performing insects, we were able to borrow two of them. *Most* fortunate! Look, there they are over there – in some ways they are better than ours for display purposes!"

Fatty was interested to hear this, as he had seen the flea-cages that very morning at the Fair. What was the name of the bad-tempered girl who owned them – Lucita? He looked along the row of display cages and recognized two that were like the one the old woman had shown him that morning. Live beetles were running about in them.

Behind the two cages was the old woman herself, duster in hand. So this was the "new job" she had spoken about to Lucita – she had taken work as a cleaner while the Conference was on. Fatty took a good look at her and wondered if *she* knew anyone with a scar that curved above his upper lip.

Fatty decided to speak to her. She would never recognize him as the boy she had seen in the flea-circus tent that morning, for he now looked totally different.

He spoke to Mr. Tolling as they leaned over the cases of scurrying beetles. "I'm sure I saw cages like these at Peterswood Fair," he said. The old woman heard him, as he meant her to.

"They'm borrowed from there," she said in her cackling voice. "They'm flea-cages from the flea-circus, young sir."

Mr. Goon loomed up majestically. "Get on with your work, woman," he said, shocked that a cleaner should talk to anyone at the Conference. The old creature gave him a sharp look out of screwed-up eyes and moved away with her duster, flicking it here and there.

"Wonderful creatures, beetles, Mr. Goon," said Fatty, in the extra-polite tones that Mr. Goon disliked and distrusted. "Have you seen the Seven-Spotted Helmeted Kicking Beetle from Ollaby-Oon in Grootenburgenstein?"

"Gah!" said Mr. Goon, and gave Fatty one of his fiercest glares. He moved away ponderously. That boy! Him and his Helmeted Beetles – that was a dig at *him*, of course, because he wore a helmet!

Mr. Tolling was extremely surprised to hear Fatty speak of a Seven-Spotted Helmeted Kicking Beetle from Ollaby-Oon in Grootenburgenstein, wherever *that* was.

"Er – that is a new kind of beetle to me," he said. "Are you sure you've got the name right, Frederick?"

"Well, it might be the *Five*-Spotted one I mean," said Fatty. "I'll just have a look round the cases and see if they've got the beetle I'm thinking of."

As Fatty had invented the beetle that very minute it was not likely that he would find it displayed anywhere, nor did he intend to look. An idea had suddenly come into his head. He moved off, leaving Mr. Tolling to gaze earnestly into every case to see if by any chance the beetle Fatty had quoted was being shown.

The old woman was dusting vigorously just behind where Goon was now standing. It had occurred to Fatty that it might be rather interesting to go over to Goon and ask him a question that might also interest the old woman, Mrs. Fangio.

"Oh – Mr. Goon – I'd just like to ask you a question, if you don't mind," said Fatty, politely.

Goon stared at him suspiciously. *Now* what was up?

"What's that?" he said.

"Well – I wondered if you had seen a man here with a thin scar curving above his upper lip," said Fatty, in a voice loud enough to reach old Mrs. Fangio, busy dusting behind the big policeman.

Mr. Goon was startled – especially as he himself had been looking out all the afternoon for exactly what Fatty had just described. So Fatty was on the same job as he was – trying to spot that escaped prisoner! *Why* had the Chief Inspector told this toad of a boy anything about the case? He began to swell with rage, and his face turned a familiar purple.

But Fatty was not watching Goon. No – he was looking closely at the old woman standing just behind. Her back had been turned when he asked the question – and for a few seconds she kept it turned, standing suddenly very still. Then she swung round and looked at him – a puzzled, half-amazed look that turned in a twinkling to an extraordinarily malevolent glare that shocked him.

Then she turned round and began dusting again, moving away as she flicked her duster here and there.

Mr. Goon was saying something to Fatty in an exasperated voice, but Fatty had no idea what it was. He had discovered what he wanted to know – that the old woman knew what he meant, just as her daughter Lucita had known – yes, both of them knew the man with the scar!

Did they also know where he was hiding? Was he in Peterswood – perhaps in the caravan colony? Well – that was something that Fatty meant to find out!

Fatty soon began to feel bored. He was longing to get back home and work out what he could do next. To his delight he discovered that Eunice was bored too.

"I thought you adored beetles," he said.

"Well, I don't," said Eunice. "Nor would you if you'd been to as many Beetle-Shows as I have. But I have to back my father up, and go with him. Can't we go off and have some tea somewhere?"

Fatty began to think that Eunice wasn't so bad after all. "But what will your father say?" he asked.

"Oh, I'll just tell him that you've kindly asked us both out to tea, and I don't want to disappoint you," said Eunice.

"But I *haven't* asked your father," said Fatty. "*Must* we? I really don't want to hear another word about beetles today or ever."

"*He* won't come," said Eunice. "Nothing will make him leave this Conference and the beetles until he's *turned* out. You'll see."

Eunice was quite right, and Fatty marched out with her, giving Mr. Goon a condescending nod as he passed him.

"Hey," said Mr. Goon, whose mind was still puzzling about Fatty's curious question to him. "Hey – a word with you, please, Master Frederick. About that man – You-Know-Who . . ."

"Another time, Goon," said Fatty, exasperatingly, and ran down the steps of the Town Hall.

"What man does the policeman mean?" asked Eunice, curiously. "Why did you speak so shortly to him – he's nice. That's the one who helped me to fight that awful old tramp the other day. The one who was in your shed, smoking a pipe – and was so violent, you know."

"Yes – *I* know," said Fatty. "I know that tramp very well indeed. As well as I know myself in fact. And he's *not* violent, nor does he smoke a pipe."

"You don't know *anything* about him!" cried Eunice. "You weren't there – you only came along afterwards."

"I was there all the time, if you'll pardon me contradicting you," said Fatty.

"I wish you wouldn't talk in riddles," said Eunice, pettishly. "You're supposed to be intelligent, but honestly no one would think it sometimes. I consider it was jolly brave of me to tackle that tramp. You're only saying that he wasn't violent just to make out that I'm not brave after all."

"Let's drop the subject," said Fatty, feeling sure that he would tell Eunice the truth about the tramp if the quarrel went on any longer. "Look – here's a tea-shop. Will this one suit Your Majesty or not?"

"I'm not going to have tea with you if you talk like that," said Eunice, beginning to be afraid that at last she had met someone who could exasperate her to tears.

"Right," said Fatty, in his extra-polite voice. "I'll go in here and have tea, and you can go into another tea-shop and have tea. I'll come in and pay your bill when you've finished. Will *that* suit you?"

Eunice glared at him and gave in. She followed him into the little tea-shop and sat down. "I'll have buttered toast and some of those cream cakes," she said.

"Jolly good idea," said Fatty, and gave the order. The waitress brought an enormous pile of buttery toast and a dish of marvellous cakes.

"I can't possibly eat all this toast," said Eunice.

"You don't have to," said Fatty. "Half is mine."

"You're slimming," said Eunice. "You surely can't be so weak-minded as to eat half that buttered toast and half those cakes!"

"Gosh – *why* do I keep on forgetting I'm slimming?" groaned Fatty, looking longingly at the two full dishes. Eunice had trapped him properly! It *would* be weak-minded to eat his share, now that she had reminded him he was slimming – and yet he couldn't bear to sit and watch her gobble up the whole lot, as she most certainly would. Greedy pig!

Then, to his enormous delight, he saw Pip and Bets passing the shop. He shot out of his seat and hurried to the door. "Pip – Bets – come on in and have some tea with me? Quick!"

In delighted surprise Pip went into the tea-shop, followed by Bets. "Eunice is here too, but you don't need to bother about her," said Fatty. "Just tuck in well, both of you!"

So they did, much to Eunice's annoyance. "Aren't *you* having any?" asked Bets, in surprise, seeing Fatty's empty plate.

"No. I'm being strong-minded about my slimming," he said, and grinned at Eunice's scowl. "Eunice and I have been to the Beetle Show. Goon was there – he tried to keep me out."

"Fatty – you didn't spot You-Know-Who, did you?" asked Bets, in a low voice. But Eunice's ears were quick, and she heard.

"Who's You-Know-Who?" she asked, with her mouth full of toast.

"I can't make out what you say when you've got your mouth full," said Fatty, reprovingly. Eunice gave a snort and emptied her mouth. "I *know* you've all got something on between you," she began. "Some secret you're not telling me. I daresay it's something silly, but it isn't good manners to keep talking secrets when I'm with you."

"We don't," said Pip, taking a cake.

"All right then – who's this You-Know-Who?" said Eunice.

"Sorry," said Fatty. "Can't tell you. Actually it's a police secret that we just happened to get to know about."

"Oooh, what a fib!" said Eunice, disbelievingly. "Police secret indeed! I don't believe it."

"Fine!" said Fatty, irritatingly. "*Don't* believe it then. That suits *us* all right."

Eunice lost her temper and went a bright red. "You're mean! You're ill-mannered! And I warn you that I shall jolly well ferret out your silly secret, whatever it is – and I'll tell everyone about it."

"Perhaps that's why we don't tell you," said Fatty, politely. "In case you do tell everyone about it. Anyway – thanks for warning us."

Eunice got up from the table and stormed out, much to the amazement of the other people in the shop. Fatty grinned at Pip and Bets. "She managed to eat a jolly good tea before she departed," he said. "Have some more cakes? Do! I'm longing to have one. I didn't dare to while Eunice was there, in case she thought I was weak-minded. But, after all, slimming doesn't mean absolutely *starving* myself!"

He ordered another plateful, and examined it closely.

"Which do you want, Bets?" he asked.

Bets laughed. "I don't mind – but I know what *you* want, Fatty!" she said, and put an éclair and a cream bun on his plate. He grinned at her.

"You always read my thoughts, young Bets," he said, and she smiled, delighted. Good old Fatty. How could that awful Eunice be so rude to him?

Fatty told Pips and Bets about his afternoon at the Beetle Conference, and the question he had asked Goon in front of Mrs. Fangio, the old woman from the Fair. "I just wanted to see if she jumped or seemed frightened, when I asked Goon about the man with the scar," he said.

"And did she?" said Pip.

"Yes. When she first heard me asking, she stood absolutely still," said Fatty.. "Then she turned round, looking really amazed – and then gave me such a wicked look! Whew! If looks could have killed, I'd be lying there dead in front of her."

"Don't say things like that, Fatty," said Bets. "Why *should* she have looked at you like that?"

91

Someone came and sat down at the next table. "Don't say any more," said Fatty. "Let's go to Larry's and all have a talk about it. Waitress – can I have the bill?"

It was quite a large bill, and for the hundredth time Pip and Bets marvelled at the amount of money Fatty always seemed to have. "Just like a grown-up," Bets thought as he paid the bill and tipped the waitress.

They all went up to Larry's, and soon the five of them, and Buster whom they had collected on the way, sat down in Larry's summer-house. Fatty told of his afternoon's doings again.

"That old woman called Mrs. Fangio, Lucita's mother, got a job as cleaner at the Town Hall this week," he said. "And I suppose when there was a difficulty over the broken beetle cases, she suggested borrowing Lucita's performing-flea cages – she would get a bit of money for that, of course. Perhaps that was what made Lucita so annoyed with her yesterday – she may have taken them without asking her."

"Quite likely," said Larry.

"Tell Larry and Daisy what happened when you asked Goon about the man with the scar," said Bets.

Fatty retold the incident. "So, you see, it's quite obvious that not only Lucita knows about the man with the scar, but her mother does too. You know I can't help wondering if they are hiding him," said Fatty.

"I'm pretty sure they are," said Larry. "Or at least they know where he *is* hiding. I wonder what relation he is to them. His photo is so like Josef – and like Lucita too – that he really must be related to them. And yet you say that Lucita said there were only she and her twin brother in her family, and her old mother. I'd ask the Chief Inspector about it, if I were you, Fatty."

"I think I will," said Fatty. "And I think that, if I possibly can, I'll slip out tonight and go down to Barker's Field and see what I can pick up about the Fangios. I'll put on my tramp clothes – what a shock for Eunice if she sees me again!"

They talked a little more, and then Fatty departed with

Buster. He debated whether to ring up the Chief Inspector at home, or from a call-box. Eunice might be somewhere about at home. But there was someone already in the public call-box so he had to wait till he got home. Then, after making sure that Eunice was not in sight, he telephoned Chief Inspector Jenks.

"Sir – it's Frederick Trotteville here," he said. "I've not got much further with that case, so far – but I want to know if you can tell me something, sir. It's about the man with a scar. I've spotted two people very like him to look at – twins – a brother and a sister, surname Fangio. But they say there aren't any others of their family, only themselves and their old mother. Could this other fellow be a cousin or some sort of relation, do you think?"

"Shouldn't think so," came back the Chief's clear voice. "He's apparently got no family, as you probably saw in those notes. His surname is Harris – or so he says. It's probably just a fluke that you saw any likeness."

"Blow!" said Fatty, and put down the receiver. "*That* clue's gone west then!*"

Adventure for Goon – and Eunice

No sooner had he put down the receiver than he heard a little scrambling noise from somewhere in the hall. Someone had been listening! Fatty hunted round, but whoever it was must have run up the stairs.

"I bet that was Eunice!" he thought. "Bother her! I didn't *really* think she meant to spy on me. I shall have to be jolly careful when I go out disguised as an old tramp again tonight!"

He gave Eunice a sharp look when he went into the dining-room for the evening meal at seven o'clock. She looked at him demurely – too demurely. He felt sure she had listened in to his telephone conversation. Still – what had she gained by it? Only that he was apparently looking for a man with a scar – who had a likeness to twins called Fangio. *That* wasn't going to help her much!

He suddenly thought of an idea and grinned as he ate his soup. "What's the joke, Frederick?" asked his mother. Fatty cast hurriedly about in his mind for some joke to tell her.

"Well, I was just remembering old Goon's face this afternoon when I asked him if he had seen the Seven-Spotted Helmeted Kicking Beetle from Ollaby-oon in Grootenburgenstein," said Fatty, much to Mr. Tolling's amazement. He put down his soup-spoon and stared at Fatty, interested.

"The Seven-Spotted *Helmeted* Beetle," he said. "I must have missed that. I really must see it tomorrow. I will ask that policeman to show me where it is."

"Yes, do," said Fatty. "He'll be interested to hear about it again."

"*Frederick!*" said his mother warningly, sure that the helmeted beetle was a make-up of Fatty's, specially thought of for the helmeted Goon.

"Yes, Mother?" said Fatty, turning an innocent gaze on Mrs. Trotteville. She shook her head at him and gave it up. But Mr. Tolling didn't. He pursued the subject of Helmeted Beetles for some time, and Fatty learnt, to his great surprise, that there really *were* "helmeted" beetles, and that apparently Mr. Tolling knew every one of them, which bored the whole table considerably.

"Shall we have another game of chess tonight?" asked Eunice, turning to Fatty as the meal ended with beetles still the subject of conversation.

"No, thanks," said Fatty, briskly. "I've got to do some cross-country running tonight. I haven't done any today, and it's a fine night. Another time, Eunice."

"I'll come with you," said Eunice. "I could do with a bit of exercise too. It's lovely running this time of the evening. I often do at home."

What a truly exasperating girl! Didn't she *know* when

she was not wanted? All right, Fatty would give her the shock of her life!

"I'll go and change into a tweed skirt and wait here for you," said Eunice, quite determined not to let Fatty out of her sight. If he thought he was going to rush off to Larry or Pip, then she was going to come too. She didn't see why she should be left out of any excitement going on.

Fatty didn't say a word. He disappeared down to his shed and hurriedly dressed himself in his tramp-clothes once more. He made up his face, stuck on the shaggy brows, and put in the prominent false teeth – and finally drew a horrible scar all down one cheek!

"The man with a scar!" he chuckled to himself. "Look out, Eunice – here he comes!"

He went out of the shed and locked the door. He stole up the garden and came to the house. He knew that his parents and Mr. Tolling had left to have a game of bridge with some friends. Only Eunice would be in the sitting-room, waiting for him.

Buster, shut up in his bedroom, was whining dolefully, as he always did when Fatty was going out without him. Eunice heard him up there, and quite thought that Fatty must be with him. She sat patiently waiting in the sitting-room, keeping a sharp ear for stealthy footsteps, in case Fatty thought of going running without her.

She heard what she was listening for – stealthy footsteps! Where did they come from? Outside the window, surely! Eunice tiptoed to the window and peered out – and there, staring at her from a bush, was the tramp – the horrible old fellow that she had seen in Fatty's shed before! But this time he had a dreadful scar running down his face. •

Eunice stared in horror! "Help!" she cried. "Here's that tramp again. Help! Frederick, where are you? That tramp's here again! Frederick!"

Jane, the house-parlourmaid, came running in at once. "What is it?" she cried. But by that time Fatty had gone from the bush. He knew that Jane's sharp eyes would recognize him through his disguise; she had seen him as an old tramp far too often!

Eunice pointed to the bush where she had seen Fatty. "He was there – that tramp again," she said. "What shall we do? Everyone's out! Where's Frederick, isn't he in his bedroom?"

"I'll go and see," said Jane. But the only occupant of Fatty's bedroom was Buster, who flew down the stairs at top speed as soon as Jane opened the door, wondering what Eunice's screams had been about.

"Master Frederick wasn't in his room," reported Jane. "He must have gone without you, Miss."

"Oh dear. I think I'd better ring up the police," said Eunice. "Yes, I must. I think somebody ought to come up and have a look round. Why, the house might be burgled tonight!"

So Eunice rang up the police, and Mr. Goon answered promptly. "Police here. Who is it?"

"This is Miss Eunice Tolling, staying with Mr. and Mrs. Trotteville," said Eunice. "I want to report seeing a horrible old tramp here – like the one I saw on Sunday."

Goon frowned. Now – what was this? He remembered Eunice perfectly, of course – but he also knew that that tramp on Sunday was *not* a tramp. And he, Goon, was NOT going on a wild tramp-chase again, not for anyone!

"Right, Miss. I'll take a few notes," said Goon. "Sorry I can't come up, but there's business here to detain me."

"But you *must* come up!" cried Eunice. "I tell you it's the same man – and I got a closer look at him this time – he's got a horrible scar on his face."

Goon got quite a shock. "A *scar*?" he said. "Are you sure?"

"Yes. Oh do come along here quickly," begged Eunice. "You might be able to catch him. Buster's in the garden too – looking for him, I expect."

That piece of news did not please Mr. Goon at all. He never liked Buster to be loose if he was anywhere near him. Still – a man with a *scar*! That really sounded some-

96

thing! Suppose he was the escaped prisoner? What a feather it would be in Goon's cap if he could catch him – *and* in that pest of a boy's own garden!

"Where's Master Frederick?" he asked.

"Out cross-country running," answered Eunice.

"Good!" thought Goon. "So *he's* out of the way. Well – I'll go up straight away."

He mounted his bicycle and pedalled up to the Trotte-villes' house. He left his bicycle just inside the front gate and went quietly round to the garden door and through it. "Miss!" he called cautiously, and gave Eunice and Jane such a fright that they both screamed loudly.

"Oh, it's you," said Jane. "What do you want to come creeping in on us like that for?"

"Well, I didn't want to give that fellow any warning," said Goon. "Now – where's this bush you saw him in, Miss? And – er – where's that dog?"

"He's still about, I think," said Jane, which made poor Goon feel very nervous indeed.

"You both come with me and we'll work through the garden," he said. "And if that dog appears, you call him, Miss. He might think I'm the tramp and go for me."

So they all three worked through the garden, poking in-to every bush. There was no sign of Buster, which delighted Goon very much.

After almost an hour's search, Goon gave it up. "That tramp's gone," he said. "Wish I knew where. I'm looking for a fellow with a scar, and it'd be a feather in my cap if I could lay my hands on him. Whereabouts was this scar, Miss? Just above his upper lip, I suppose?"

"Oh no – all down one cheek," said Eunice in surprise. "Whatever made you think it was just above his mouth?"

Goon stared at her, bitterly disappointed and really angry. "But – but I thought you meant – oh well, I suppose you couldn't know where the scar ought to be. Blow it – it's not the man I thought it was. It must have been – oh *no*! – yes, it *must* have been that toad of a boy disguised

97

again! And you said he'd gone *running*! What do you mean by telling me such fairy tales!"

Eunice stared at the angry policeman in dismay. "I don't know what you're talking about," she said. "And I will *not* be talked to like this. I shall go to bed."

And away she went, holding her head high. How DARE that horrid policeman speak to her like that.

Jane laughed. "There goes Miss High-and-Mighty!" she said. "You look hot and bothered, Mr. Goon, sir. You come along into my kitchen and I'll make you a cup of tea, and give you one of Cookie's shortbread biscuits. For all we know, Miss Eunice didn't see anyone at all – just a moving shadow!"

Mr. Goon removed his helmet, wiped his hot head and graciously accepted Jane's invitation. He sat in her kitchen enjoying himself, telling her tales of his valour, and of the numberless arrests he had made. He didn't hear quiet footsteps coming to the lighted kitchen window. He didn't see a scarred face peering in at him. He didn't even guess that Fatty had come back, still in his tramp clothes, and was even now getting out of them down in the shed.

Goon suddenly caught sight of the kitchen clock and was horrified to see the time. "I must go. Where's my helmet?" he said. "My word, how the time's gone. Goodnight to you, Miss, and thank you."

He blundered out into the garden and went to find his bicycle. To his consternation it was gone! "I *know* I left it just here – and it's gone! It's been stolen!" he said. "That fathead of a girl is the cause of this – bringing me away from all my work to hunt someone I thought was the man with the scar. Gah! Now I've got to walk home."

And walk home he did – only to find the telephone ringing as soon as he got in. NOW who wanted him? If it was *another* tale about a tramp, he'd let fly!

But it was Fatty's smooth confident voice. "Is that you, Mr. Goon? I have to report that there is a bicycle leaning by our kitchen door. I don't know whose it is, but possibly you have had one reported to you as stolen."

"You – you pest!" shouted Goon into the telephone. "You found my bike by your front gate, I know you did – and you took it away and hid it till I left – and now it's by your kitchen door, you say. Well, WHO put it there? That's what *I* want to know. WHO put it there?"

But there was no answer except a chuckle. The phone went dead, and Goon groaned. Now he had got to walk all the way back and fetch his bicycle! All right, Master Frederick Trotteville, you just wait – you'll get paid out one day!

Fatty Has a Surprise

While Mr. Goon and Eunice and Jane had been searching feverishly for the old tramp, Fatty had been having quite an interesting time. He had hurriedly left his garden by the little gate at the bottom, as soon as he heard Goon coming on his bicycle. Then he had made his way towards the river.

"Barker's Field is the one near old Barker's farmhouse," he thought. "If I meet anyone in this tramp get-up, I'll ask if they can tell me of any old barn I'd be allowed to sleep in. Gosh – what a scream Eunice let out when she saw my face peeping out of that bush! I hope Goon and she had a wonderful time hunting all through the garden!"

He put on a limp whenever he met anyone, and suddenly decided to cut himself a stick from the hedgerow. He could use it as a walking-stick – and it might come in useful if there were any loose dogs at the caravan camp.

He cut himself quite a stout hazel staff, and set off again. He came at last to the caravan field and stood looking at it. Which caravan was the Fangios'? There were about twenty caravans standing about, some modern, some old. Most of them had lights on inside.

No one seemed to be about, so Fatty grew quite bold.

He peeped into a nearby caravan

He peeped into a nearby caravan, standing on one of the wheels to reach the window. The curtains were pulled across but a crack had been left between them. Two people sat inside, one sewing, one reading. Man and wife, probably, quite decent-looking people.

He went to the next caravan – a very modern one. A dog barked as he came near, and Fatty decided he wouldn't go any further. He crossed the field and came to an old caravan that badly needed repainting. The night was now coming down quickly, and Fatty pulled out his torch. There was no light in this van. Perhaps it was empty?

It was. It smelt musty as he opened the door, and he shut it again quickly. Pooh! He went down the steps and looked round again. This sort of thing wasn't going to get him very far!

As he went to yet another caravan, someone came down the steps and spotted him in the darkness. "Who's there?" called a man's voice.

"Only an old fellow who wants a doss-down somewhere," said Fatty, in a high cracked voice. "Can you tell me if there's a hay-stack anywhere, Mister?"

"Come in here and we'll give you a cup of tea," said the voice. "The farmer doesn't like tramps. He'll set his dog on you if you go on to his land. Let's have a look at you."

Fatty limped up the caravan steps. It was an old caravan, but the inside was fairly clean, though not very comfortable. The man who had spoken to him was an oldish fellow with a kindly face. Inside was another old man.

"My brother," said the first man. "He's blind. We make pegs and baskets to sell, and we ain't got much money, but we can always spare a cup of tea. Can't we, Steve?"

"Ay," said the blind man, and put out his hands to clear away a mess of cane and half-made baskets near him. "Set you down."

Soon Fatty was sitting down drinking a very strong cup of tea. "I'm looking for some people called the Fangios," he said. "Do you know them? I was told they had a caravan here."

"Oh ay," said the first man. "Their caravan is over yonder."

"Two of them, there are," said the blind man. "Brother and sister."

"No, three now," said the brother. "An old woman, their mother. Proper old tartar she is, and strong as a horse. Chops up all the wood, and carries buckets of water as good as any man! Her daughter, Lucita, she's a sulky young woman, she is, but the brother's all right."

"Yes – that's Josef," said the blind man. "He takes my baskets to fairs for me, when they're around about here, or to the market, and sells them. He's a good lad. Are they relations of yours?"

"Not exactly," said Fatty. "They wouldn't know me now. I'm a lot different from the last time they saw me! Ah, this tea's good – black and strong, how I like it!"

"We've got a loaf and some marge if you want a bite," said the blind man. "Cut him a bit, Bill."

"No, thanks," said Fatty, hurriedly, touched by the generosity of this poor old couple. Bill turned up the wick of the lamp a little, and looked at Fatty, sizing him up.

"You can sleep here in our van if you so wish," he said, after a moment.

"Well, thanks all the same – but I think I'll be getting on," said Fatty. "That tea was just what I wanted!"

"You got a queer scar there, above your mouth," said Bill. "Like a snake! How did you get that?"

"Blow!" thought Fatty. "I forgot I'd painted on that wonderful scar!" He laughed, and answered the old fellow. "Oh, that's nothing. Can't go through life without a few scars – that's right, ain't it, Bill?"

A small noise came from outside the caravan, and the blind man lifted his head. "That's that old cat," he said. "Let it in, Bill."

Bill opened the door and a thin tabby cat came in, with
102

bitten ears. "Is this yours?" asked Fatty. "It looks half-starved."

"Nay, it's not ours," said Bill, pouring a little milk into a saucer. "It belongs to them Fangios, but it seems to me they don't never feed the poor critter."

Fatty watched the cat lap up the milk and an idea came into his head.

"I'll take it to the Fangios' caravan if you'll show me which it is," he said.

They let the cat finish the milk and then Fatty picked it up. It would be a marvellous way of having a look into the Fangios' caravan if he took back their cat!"

The old couple bade him good-night, pointing out the Fangios' caravan, a fairly big, quite modern one, and then shut their door. Carrying the mewing cat, Fatty went over towards the caravan.

As he came near, the door opened and a voice called out "Puss, Puss, Puss – come along in!"

"Oh, good!" thought Fatty. "That sounds like Josef." As he came near a figure ran down the caravan steps, still calling.

"I've got your cat!" called Fatty. "I'm bringing it." Someone came up to him, a dark shadow in the star-lit night, and felt for the cat.

Fatty switched on his torch. It was old Mrs. Fangio, not Josef. "Now, Minnie, Minnie," she said, and took the cat. "Did Jo and Lucita turn you out, then, the bad ones?"

"Minnie came over to Bill's caravan," said Fatty. "They gave her some milk."

The old woman fondled the scrawny cat and Fatty waited in hopes of being asked into the caravan. He was longing to have a good look round it to see if there was anyone else there besides the Fangio twin, but no invitation came. Instead the old woman turned her back and went back to the caravan without another word. Fatty switched on his torch so that she could see to get up the steps. She certainly looked a dirty untidy old woman, and Fatty smiled to see the enormous old carpet slippers she was wearing, as she went up the steps, clutching the cat. She didn't even say good-night to him, but slammed the door quickly.

He waited a little while in the darkness, and then he sidled towards the caravan. He meant to look in at one of the windows. If only there was a crack to see through, he might spot something interesting – maybe a fourth person – *with a scarred face!*

But the curtains were drawn tightly across. Not a chink had been left. Fatty was bitterly disappointed. He was standing on the big wheel, and was just about to get down when he heard voices – angry voices – coming from the caravan.

He listened, but the window was shut and he could not make out the words. Blow! And then suddenly he stiffened and held his breath.

There was a woman's voice – that would be Lucita's – or maybe old Mrs. Fangios' – and there were two men's voices – *two!* One shouted something, and before he had finished another man's voice began to shout back. There was a quarrel going on – and two of the quarrellers were men! Could one be the man with a scar? How Fatty longed to be able to peep in and see!

He suddenly had a shock. Someone came across the field, and walked right up to the Fangios' caravan. Whoever it was rapped at the door. Fatty simply didn't know what to do – there he was, perched on the high wheel, not daring to jump down in case the visitor saw him. He decided to stay where he was.

Someone opened the door. "Who is it?" said Lucita's voice.

"It's Fred. Ask Josef if he's coming with us – we're going to have a game of darts."

"Josef – Fred wants you," called Lucita. She turned back to Fred. "I'll come with you too," she said. "I'm sick of being cooped up in this caravan."

104

And, while Fatty was still perched precariously on the wheel, the three went off across the field together. Now, thought Fatty, only the old woman – and the other man, whoever he was – were in the van. HOW could Fatty have a peep and see? He got down quietly from the wheel, and was about to go round by the door to see if by any chance it had been left open, when someone came down the steps. Fatty crouched back into the shadows. Who was it? The old woman – or the second man?

He couldn't see. The figure went quickly away into the darkness and was lost. Fatty blundered after it for a few paces, but gave it up. No – he would go and peep into the caravan and see who was left there! If anyone saw him and came after him he would take to his heels and run. But he MUST see who was there!

He went quickly up the steps. The caravan door was shut, but he didn't think it could be locked because he had not heard a key being turned. He took the handle and began to turn it very slowly.

Then he pushed at the door and opened it inch by inch. There was not a sound from inside. Fatty was quite ready to leap down the steps and run off at top speed at the first sound!

He got the door half ajar, and still there was no sound. Then he flung it wide open, meaning to take a quick look round, spot who was there, and race off.

The door swung right back and Fatty looked swiftly into the untidy van. There were two sleeping-bunks, one above the other, and an old mattress rolled up below one – a folding table, two chairs and an oil-stove. An oil-lamp hung from the roof, giving quite a good light.

But there was nobody there! Fatty stood on the top step, raking the van from corner to corner with startled eyes. There seemed nowhere for anyone to hide – well, then, where was the fourth person he had heard shouting?

Fatty was so astonished that he quite forgot that he could easily be seen by anyone outside the caravan, outlined clearly against the light from inside. And suddenly there came a yell.

"Hey – who's that at the Fangios' van? Hey you – what you doing?"

Fatty tells his Tale

Fatty just had time to leap down the steps and run for his life before two men from the next caravan came at him. He tore over the grass towards the gate that led out of the field.

The men chased him, shouting. Fatty suddenly caught his foot in something and fell headlong. The men gained on him at once, and just as he got up, one of them shone a torch on him.

"Get him, quick!" he shouted – but before either of the men could grab him something leapt out of the darkness, snarling and growling – something small and fierce.

It was Buster! He had trailed Fatty all the way from his house down to the field. Now he threw himself into the fray, snarling so fiercely, and giving such nasty little nips, that the two men drew back in fear.

Fatty raced off again, and Buster followed, pausing every now and again to look back at the two angry men. They made no attempt to go after Fatty.

"He was going to rob the Fangios' van," said one. "We'd better report him to the police. Did you get a look at him? What a nasty bit of work!"

"Yes, I saw him clearly," said the other man. "He'd got a scar down his face – did you see it? I'd know him again all right if ever I saw him."

Fatty didn't stop running till he was well away from Barker's Field. Then, panting, he sat down on a roadside seat, and made a fuss of the delighted Buster.

"You couldn't have come at a more convenient moment,"

he said. "I really was in a bad spot, Buster. Those men would have yanked me off to old Goon, I bet they would! Whew! I nearly broke my leg when I fell down. I shall have a bruise the size of a saucer tomorrow. Well, come on, Buster old thing. Thanks a lot for tracking me so well!'"

Fatty went the rest of the way slowly, his leg paining him. He was quite glad of the hazel stick he had cut! His pretended limp had become a real one.

He talked quietly to Buster as he went along. "You know, Buster, old fellow, this has been quite an exciting evening – but I'm blessed if I know what to make of things. I feel sure that the man with a scar is being hidden by the Fangios – but WHERE? I heard his voice in the caravan, I'm sure I did. *Could* I have been mistaken? No, I don't think so."

"Wuff," said Buster, sympathetically. "Wuff, wuff."

"I've a feeling that *all* the Fangios are in the plot," said Fatty. "And I've a feeling too that they're all angry about it for some reason. Don't they want to hide the fellow with a scar? If so, why are they doing so? For money? Perhaps he was in prison for stealing, and hid the money before he was caught. Perhaps now he's out he's hoping to get it when the coast is clear – and won't tell the other three where it is? But where on earth is he *hiding*?"

Fatty got back to his shed at last, stripped off his disguise, cleaned his face and went indoors to have a bath. He was thankful to see that Eunice had gone to bed. His parents and Mr. Tolling were not yet home.

He rolled into bed at last, Buster beside him in his basket. Fatty let his hand hang down from the bed so that Buster could lick it good-night.

"You're a good friend, Buster," said Fatty, sleepily. "Good-night. I want to think things out but I'm too tired. My brain isn't working. I'll have to call a meeting tomorrow and let the others do some thinking!"

But the others were no better than Fatty at solving the tangle that this particular mystery had got into! Hearing that Eunice was going out with his mother that morning,

Fatty promptly rang up Larry and Pip and ordered a meeting sharp at ten o'clock down in his shed.

They all came punctually, anxious to know what had happened. Fatty had lemonade and biscuits ready, and they sat down prepared for a most interesting time. NOW what had Fatty been up to?

"Well," began Fatty, "you know that I planned to go down to Barker's Field and see if I could gather any information there, don't you? Actually I did get quite a lot but unfortunately I can't make head or tail of it. So we'll *all* have to set our brains to work and find out what's happening."

"Go on, then," said Larry. "We won't interrupt."

Fatty began his tale, telling first of all how he had scared poor Eunice by appearing in his tramp clothes again, plus a scar down his face! When he related how she had telephoned Goon and made him cycle up to the house, they all roared.

Fatty went on with his tale. "Well, I went down to the field. First of all I went to a caravan where two nice old men lived, and they gave me a cup of tea and told me where the Fangios' caravan was. And would you believe it, while I was there, I had a real bit of luck, because the Fangios' scrawny old cat came mewing up their steps for some milk!"

"Gosh – so you took the chance of taking it over to the Fangios' caravan, I suppose?" said Pip.

"Quite right," said Fatty. "I went over to it, carrying the cat. When I got near I heard someone calling for the cat and I thought it was Josef, but it was old Mrs. Fangio shouting 'Minnie, Minnie!' I gave her the cat and hoped she would ask me into the caravan, but she didn't. I switched on my torch to light the old woman up the steps of the caravan, but she never even said thank you. Gosh, she did look a sight with her dirty old shawl and carpet slippers on her feet, waddling up the steps! Anyway – bang went the caravan door and that was that."

"What happened next?" asked Bets, listening to every word, and thinking how well Fatty could tell a story!

"Well, I thought I'd stand on a wheel and peep into the caravan," said Fatty, "and just see if a fourth person was there, and if so whether he had a scar or not! So up I got, but the curtains were too closely pulled. I was just going to get down when a quarrel began in the van. I heard the old woman's voice – or it might have been Lucita's – and I also heard TWO men's voices!"

"I *say*!" said Pip, his eyes shining. "Did you really? Who was the other fellow, then?"

"I don't know. Anyway, there was a fine old quarrel, with shouts and yells," said Fatty. "In the middle of it someone came over to the caravan, and rapped on the door. I was scared stiff – but it was only somebody called Fred who wanted Josef to go and have a game of darts with him. The quarrel inside the van stopped, and Josef – and Lucita too – went off with Fred."

"So the old woman and the second man were left in the caravan?" said Daisy.

"Yes. Well, I got down off the wheel after a bit – and just then someone came out of the caravan and went quietly down the steps!"

"Who was it?" asked everyone.

"I couldn't see – it was maddening!" said Fatty. "I daren't switch on my torch, of course. Anyway, it had to be either old Mrs. Fangio or the other man. So I made up my mind I'd open the caravan door and take a quick look in to see who was left alone there – the old woman or the man – and *perhaps* it would be the man with the scar!"

"Gosh!" said Larry. "This is jolly exciting. Buck up – what happened?"

"Well, I *did* open the door," said Fatty, "and I did look all round the van – and believe it or not, there was nobody there! The van was empty. And I'm *certain* there was no-where that a person could hide without my seeing them."

There was an astonished silence. "But, Fatty," said Larry, "you *must* have been mistaken in some way. I mean
109

– if old Mrs. Fangio and the other man were in the van together, and only one went out, the other was still left. That's only common sense."

"*I* know!" said Pip. "You thought you only saw *one* person going out, after Josef and Lucita had left – but probably in the darkness there were *two* – going off very quietly in case someone saw them."

Fatty hesitated. "It does seem the only explanation," he said. "But I'm pretty certain that only three people left that caravan – and yet the fourth disappeared also. I can tell you, I was pretty puzzled."

"What did you do next?" asked Bets.

"Well, someone saw me outlined against the light in the Fangios' van, thought I was a thief and came after me. I took to my heels, of course, and raced off. Then I caught my foot in something and crashed to the ground – my word, I've got a bruise on my leg this morning. Look!"

Everyone exclaimed at the enormous black bruise that Fatty very proudly displayed. "The men didn't catch you, did they?" asked Bets, anxiously.

"No. But it was a very near thing," said Fatty. "Old Buster turned up at that very moment – and my word he scared the men so thoroughly that I was able to get up and race off at top speed! You should have heard him snarling! Talk about a fierce dog – he sounded like an Alsatian, a Labrador and a Scottie all rolled into one!"

"Good old Buster," said Bets, patting him. "What a good thing he turned up. I suppose he trailed you all the way there, Fatty."

"Yes. Eunice must have let him out of my bedroom," said Fatty. "Good thing she did! I might have been languishing in a cell down at the police-station by now! Well – what do you make of all that? Anyone got any ideas?"

Nobody said a word for a minute or two. They were turning Fatty's story over and over in their minds. It was certainly rather a curious one!

"I still think that *two* people must have left the van together, after Josef and Lucita had gone," said Pip at last.

"And I think too that the second man in the van – the man whose voice you heard quarrelling with Josef – may very likely have been the man with the scar."

"I think that too," said Larry, and the others agreed.

"Right. What do we do next?" asked Fatty. Before anyone could answer, Buster began to bark loudly and then ran to the door.

"Someone's outside," said Pip. "I bet it's Eunice!"

It was – a very annoyed Eunice too. "Why didn't you tell me there was a meeting down in your shed, Frederick?" she demanded. "Why do you leave me out of things? Surely you could let me share in what you're doing, just for a few days? And WHY did you go off running without me last night? That awful old tramp came back – and Mr. Goon came, and was very rude to me."

"Sorry, Eunice," said Fatty. "Well, do join us – have a spot of lemonade and a biscuit!"

The others glanced at one another. Had Eunice overheard anything of Fatty's story? Well, she wouldn't have been able to make much of it, if she had. They looked at Fatty, pouring out lemonade very politely.

What was he going to do next? This mystery seemed to be in a fine old tangle!

Goon is a Nuisance

Eunice then began to tell everyone all about her fright over the tramp the night before, and described the horrible scarred face that the man had. They listened politely, longing to laugh, knowing that it had only been Fatty in disguise again. In the middle of the story Jane came and knocked at the door.

"Please, Master Frederick, it's the policeman, Mr. Goon, to see you," she said.

"Blow!" said Fatty, getting up. "It's about that tramp,

111

I suppose. Eunice, you'd better come with us. After all, *you* saw him. I didn't."

"Don't you let Mr. Goon be rude to me, Frederick, will you?" said Eunice.

"I will certainly see that he treats you with the utmost respect," said Fatty, firmly. "But just you stand up for yourself, Eunice – don't let him make out that that tramp is all a fairy-tale of yours."

"It's a great pity Jane didn't see him too," she said. "Look, there's Mr. Goon."

Goon was waiting on the path that led up to the house. He was not going to let Fatty slip away. Oh no – he had had important news that morning, that tied up with the old scarred tramp that that girl Eunice had said she'd seen last night. He had changed his ideas now about the tramp being Fatty, but he wanted to be quite sure about it. He had, in fact, wanted only a quiet word with Fatty, and he was annoyed when he saw Eunice and the others too.

"Er – can I have a word with you, Master Frederick?" he said. "Alone?"

"What about?" said Fatty. "If it's about the tramp last night, you must ask Miss Eunice here – she saw him."

"Yes, I certainly did see him," said Eunice. "And what is more, as I told you last night, Constable, Frederick had gone off on some cross-country running. *He* can't tell you anything about that tramp, because he wasn't here."

"Yes, yes, I see," said Goon. "So you went off running, did you, Master Frederick, you didn't spend the evening at home?"

"Good gracious no, Goon," said Fatty, sounding surprised. "I was miles away."

"Ah – that was one thing I wanted to be sure of," said Goon. "You see – I half thought *you* might have been that old tramp Miss Eunice here said she saw."

"*Well!*" said Eunice, in a rage. "Do you suppose I'm such an idiot as not to be able to tell whether a tramp is a tramp, or whether he's Frederick Trotteville? I tell you, HE – WAS – A – TRAMP, Mr. Goon. A horrible fellow. Very like the one

112

I saw on Sunday, except that he had a scar."

"Ah – that's what I wanted to know too," said Goon, taking out his notebook. "Now – did you notice very, very carefully exactly how big the scar was, and what position it was in?"

"Well, I didn't go out and get hold of the tramp's chin, and peer at the scar, or take a ruler to measure it, if that's what you mean!" said Eunice. "I was in too great a fright to do anything but *notice* it."

"Ah – so long as you noticed he was *scarred*!" said Goon. "I had a report from somewhere else last night to say that there was a tramp trying to break in, with intent to steal – and *that* tramp had a scar on his face too! So you can see, Miss, why I'm glad that you spotted that *your* tramp had one too!"

"Don't call him *my* tramp!" said Eunice, annoyed. "Well, fancy that fellow going on somewhere else to break in. It *must* be the same tramp. He certainly did have a scarred face."

Fatty had become very interested. Was this tramp with the scar, who had been reported for breaking in somewhere, no other than Fatty himself – reported by the two men who had seen him opening the door of the Fangios' caravan? Or was he quite another scarred man, from somewhere else – possibly the prisoner they were after.

"Goon," said Fatty, "where was this fellow trying to break in last night?"

"Never you mind," said Goon, irritatingly. "But from what I've heard he's certainly the fellow we're after. That scar proves it. He'd have been caught last night all right by the men who reported him, but for a dog that came out of nowhere and attacked them."

"Aha!" thought Fatty. "That was old Buster. So *I* was the 'tramp' those two men reported. Goon *hasn't* got hold of the right man, thank goodness. But he's hot on the trail, though he doesn't know it – because I'm pretty certain the real scarred man *is* being sheltered by the Fangios, down in that caravan camp. What a pity the two men reported me

– now Goon will be searching the camp himself, and being a policeman, he can do it much better than I can!"

"Do you want to ask me any more questions?" said Eunice, tired of watching the policeman write voluminously in his notebook.

"No, thank you, Miss," said Goon. "You've put me on the right trail, I think. I'll just get my bike and be off. That reminds me – HOW did my bike take itself out of your front garden and put itself by your kitchen door last night, Master Frederick?"

"I'll work it out when I've got time," said Fatty, with a perfectly straight face. "Was it trying to come to look for you in the kitchen, do you think?"

"Gah!" said Goon in disgust. "You'll cut yourself one day, you're so sharp!"

And away he went up the path, hoping sincerely that his bicycle hadn't disappeared again!

"What do you suppose Goon is going to do now?" asked Pip.

"I *imagine* that he'll ask Chief Inspector Jenks for a search-warrant and a couple of men – and go and search the caravan camp in Barker's Field," said Fatty gloomily. "And as I think that that man with a scar *must* be there somewhere, Goon is likely to pull him in. And *I* put him on to the right place to search by being ass enough to get caught by those two men last night!"

"What *is* all this?" said Eunice, puzzled.

"Oh, gosh – I forgot you were here, Eunice," said Fatty. "Well – I suppose we'll *have* to tell you something of what is going on, or you'll keep on worrying us."

"I certainly shall," said Eunice. "I must say I think you're pretty mean to keep things secret, especially when that old tramp I saw has something to do with it. I shall go and ask your mother what's happening, if you don't tell me."

"Tell-tale," murmured Pip, and got a furious look from Eunice. "Frederick," she said, "tell me, please. I'll help you

114

if I can. You seem to be doing some kind of detective work – and I'm good at that too."

Fatty groaned. "Is there anything you're *not* good at, Eunice?" he asked. "Now listen – briefly, this is how things stand. There's an escaped prisoner, with a scarred face, somewhere in the district. He's actually been seen. We have been keeping a look-out for him, but we haven't been lucky, so far. We were told to look for him in crowds, where perhaps he might not be noticed – the Fair, for instance – and even the Beetle Meetings, as one of his interests is insects."

"Oh! I might have sat next to him!" said Eunice, quite scared. "What's he like? I've gathered that he has a scar on his face, of course."

"He's got sharp eyes," said Pip, "And a thin mouth . . ."

"And thick dark hair," said Larry. "And he's medium height."

"And his hands are very knobbly and bony," said Daisy. "And . . ."

"And we feel that possibly some people called the Fangios, who run the flea-circus at the Fair, and also the shooting-range, may be hiding him," said Fatty. "Because they go all peculiar when we mention men with scarred faces! Even that old cleaner-woman at the Beetle Show, who is also a Fangio, got a shock when I mentioned a man with a scar."

"I see," said Eunice. "Yes, I remember that old woman. Where does she live? At the Fair?"

"No, the Fangios have a caravan down in Barker's Field," said Fatty. "And what we're afraid of now is that Goon is on the same trail as we are – though not for the same reason – and may search that camp and get *our* man! What a feather in his helmet, if so."

"I don't like that policeman," said Eunice. "I'm on your side. I'd like to help, Frederick. What are your plans?"

"Well," said Fatty, "let's go down to the shed again. I don't know that we've really got any plans yet."

So Eunice went down to the shed with the others, quite

determined to show them that she was as good a detective as any of them.

It proved difficult to think of a really good plan, but at last they decided that if Goon *did* get a search-warrant for the camp, they simply must be there too. At least they must be in at the finish, even if Goon won the victory!

"What's the time?" said Fatty. "Gosh, the morning's nearly gone! Listen – Goon can't get a search-warrant before this afternoon. One or other of us must haunt Barker's Field the whole time, from say two o'clock onwards, so that warning can be sent to the rest of us if Goon arrives with other policemen."

"Yes. That's a good idea," said Pip. "We can watch two at a time, so that there is always one to send off to warn the others. I'll watch with Bets. We can pretend to be picnicking, or something."

"And I'll watch with Larry," said Daisy.

"And I'll watch with you, Frederick," said Eunice.

"You can't," said Fatty. "You've got to go to the Beetle Conference. And if you do, just keep an eye on that old cleaner-woman, will you – Mrs. Fangio."

"I *wish* I hadn't to go to this afternoon's meeting," said Eunice. "I'd much rather be with you. Who will you send to tell the others, Frederick, if anything happens while you are watching?"

"Buster," said Fatty. "I can tie a note to his collar and just say 'Go to Larry' and he'll be off like a shot. And Larry could phone Pip."

"Oh yes – I suppose you *could* do that," said Eunice. "Well – I'll try and take my turn with you after tea, Frederick, then you won't be alone. I say – this is rather exciting, isn't it?"

"*I* don't think so," said poor Fatty. "It's bad enough to come to a full-stop, just when you've got some interesting clues – but it's worse to have someone like Goon going over your head, and winning by accident, so to speak!"

"Bets and I will be at the field at two o'clock," said Pip. "Larry, you relieve us at four, and bring your tea. Then

Fatty can have his turn after tea with Eunice."

"Right. See you all later," said Fatty, and the meeting ended. Fatty watched them all leaving the shed. "The fun's over," he thought. "Goon's really holding the reins now although he doesn't know it!"

Watching and Waiting

Eunice went off to the Beetle Meeting that afternoon with her father. Mr. Tolling was quite disappointed that Fatty didn't want to come as well. But Fatty was firm.

"I really must do a few jobs for my mother," he said. He felt that he could not listen to any more Beetle Talk. Mr. Tolling had lectured them during the whole of lunch-time on the extraordinary habits of the Family of Gulping Beetles of Ruahua in New Zealand. He only stopped when Fatty began to make the most peculiar swallowing noises, which alarmed his mother considerably.

"Frederick – are you choking?" she said, anxiously, half getting up from her chair.

"No, Mother, no – it's listening to all that about the Gulping Beetles," said Fatty, faintly. "I can't seem to stop gulping myself."

Eunice gave a squeal of laughter, but Mr. Tolling could not see anything funny at all. Fatty caught his mother's stern eye and stopped gulping. He was very, very glad when at last Mr. Tolling, complete with umbrella and gloves, and attended by Eunice, left for the Town Hall.

"I'll keep an eye on that woman!" hissed Eunice to Fatty, as they left, causing her father to gaze at her in surprise. What woman? And what *was* Eunice looking so excited about? Really, she was getting as bad as that boy Frederick!

Pip and Bets were down in Barker's Field just before

two o'clock. They had decided to take their books on wild flowers, and to hunt for some. Then, when they had a bunch, they could perhaps sit down somewhere near the Fangios' caravan and keep a watch in case Goon came.

Nobody bothered about them at all, and nothing happened of any interest. They just sat there, not far from the Fangios' caravan, pretending to look at their flower-books. The caravan was shut, and nobody seemed to be there.

"I expect that girl Lucita has gone to the Fair to show off her performing fleas," said Pip. "And the young man – what was his name – Josef – is looking after the shooting-range."

"And old Ma Fangio will be dusting away at the Beetle Conference," said Bets. "This would be quite a good time for Goon to come and search their caravan. I wonder if there is anyone hiding in there this very minute!"

"They're jolly quiet, if so," said Pip.

At four o'clock Larry and Daisy came along to take their turn and Pip and Bets departed. Nothing happened while Larry and Daisy were there, either. They picnicked, chatted with a small child who came wandering up, and read their books. They kept an eye on the caravan, but nobody went in or out at all. Goon did not appear either. Altogether, it was really rather dull. They were glad when Fatty turned up with Eunice.

"Nothing to report," said Larry. "And Pip had no news either. How long will you sit here, Fatty? When do you think Goon will come – if he does come?"

"I don't know. But I think if he hasn't come by seven, I'll ring up the Chief Inspector and see if Goon *is* trying to get a search-warrant," said Fatty. "It would be a help to know."

"Right," said Larry. "Well, good luck. Give me a ring if you want me to come down after our evening meal, and keep watch."

"Thanks," said Fatty.

"Isn't this *fun*?" said Eunice, as she settled down in the

grass near Fatty. But Fatty was in a gloomy mood and didn't respond at all. The Fangio caravan still remained shut, and was silent and apparently empty. Fatty began to wonder if his reasoning had been all wrong. Was he correct in thinking that the scarred man was being hidden by the Fangios?

"After all, the only *real* clue we have is the fact that Lucita and Josef both look rather like the photo of the man with a scar," thought Fatty, "and Lucita seemed surprised and angry when I mentioned a scarred man – and so did her mother. But that's absolutely the only reason why I think they may be hiding the fellow. It seems pretty thin reasoning really."

Eunice soon got bored with Fatty. "I'll take a look round the camp," she said, getting up. "I'm bored sitting here."

"No, don't wander about," said Fatty. "You'll only draw attention to us. Sit down again. Tell me about the meeting this afternoon."

"There's nothing to tell," said Eunice, rather sulkily. "I saw that cleaner-woman. I watched her all the time to see if she did anything suspicious."

"But how *could* she do anything suspicious? Don't be silly," said Fatty.

"Well, she might have. You told me to keep an eye on her," argued Eunice. "So I did. She stared back at me – in fact we had quite a staring-match. I don't like her."

"Well, look – here she comes!" said Fatty, suddenly. "Don't stare though – she may recognize you. Eunice, I said *don't* stare!"

But Eunice did. Mrs. Fangio was coming over the field, her shawl over her dirty grey hair, and her wrinkled face as brown as a berry. She saw Eunice, as she came near the caravan.

"Ho! So you're here, are you!" she said. "What did you stare at me for all the afternoon? *I* saw you – rude little pig!"

"Don't talk to me like that," said Eunice, in her high-and-mighty way.

"And just get away from here!"

"I'll talk to you how I like," said Mrs. Fangio, who seemed to be in a very bad temper. "And just get away from here, see? This is a caravan camp, and you've got no business here, no, nor that boy neither. You can clear out, both of you."

"Well, we shan't," said Eunice. "How dare you talk to me like that!"

"I'll show you!" said Mrs. Fangio, and she came quickly up to where Eunice sat. Fatty leapt up, afraid that the angry old woman was going to hit Eunice. He caught her arm as she raised it.

"Now!" he said, "there's no need for . . ." But he didn't finish what he was going to say, for the angry old woman hit him such a blow on the chin that he fell backwards, landing heavily on the squealing Eunice. Mrs. Fangio gave a strange, hoarse laugh and went up the steps of the caravan, unlocking it with a key.

"Oh, Frederick – you squashed all the breath out of me!" cried Eunice. "Get off! What are you doing?"

Fatty slid off the angry girl, feeling considerably astonished. What a good thing he had caught that blow and not Eunice. He felt his chin tenderly. Bad-tempered old woman! Fatty heard the sound of laughter, and saw two or three children nearby, pointing at him.

"She gave you one all right!" said a small boy. "And down you went!"

"Plonk!" added a small girl.

"Come on, Eunice. Let's get away from here," said Fatty, feeling most humiliated. The old woman had taken him quite by surprise. To think he had gone down flat like that! Fatty hoped that Eunice would hold her tongue about it.

"I'm going back home," announced Eunice. "I've had enough of this. Horrible old woman! She might set the son and daughter on us too, when they come back. This is a silly idea of yours, Frederick."

"All right. We'll go back," said Fatty, quite shaken. They walked by the small children, who sent a volley of squeals after them. Eunice was longing to tick them off but Fatty wouldn't let her.

"Now just you shut up for a bit," he said. "If you hadn't stared at that old woman when I told you not to, this wouldn't have happened."

"You hurt me when you fell on me," Eunice complained. "Do you mean to say you fell down because that silly old woman hit you? Well!"

"She just got in a lucky blow, that I wasn't expecting," said Fatty. "Now do be quiet, Eunice. I want to think."

As soon as they got back, Fatty rang up the Chief Inspector. "Frederick Trotteville here, sir. Er – I wonder if you'd tell me if Mr. Goon has got in touch with you recently about the escaped prisoner case, sir? Several things have happened, and. . ."

"Yes. I know. And Goon wanted a warrant to search a caravan camp," said the Inspector's voice. "I said he could have one tomorrow. Have you unearthed any fresh news about the case, Frederick?"

"Well no, sir," said poor Fatty. "I mean – I've got clues that just don't seem to lead anywhere. I can't help thinking that the only thing to do *is* to search the camp."

"Right," said the business-like voice at the other end of the line. "Sorry about it, Frederick, if you were hoping to solve the case. But you can't always be successful, you know. Good-bye."

Poor Fatty. He felt very down in the dumps as he went in to the evening meal that night, and nobody could get a word out of him. Eunice offered to play chess with him afterwards.

"No, thanks," said Fatty, feeling quite certain she would beat him tonight, "I'm going up to bed soon."

"Good *gracious*!" said Eunice, surprised. "By the way, how's your chin?" She gave a most annoying little giggle.

"Well, if you really want to know, it's jolly sore!" said Fatty, fiercely. "It's black and blue. And stop that idiotic giggling."

"What a fuss to make about being hit by a poor old

122

woman," said Eunice, mockingly. "Cheer up! You're *really* going to bed, I suppose, Frederick? You're not going to slip out again for anything exciting, are you?"

"As if I'd tell you!" said Fatty, and went upstairs with Buster, leaving Eunice wondering if he *did* mean to slip out again after all. Well – she would keep a watch and if he did, she would follow him. That would serve him right for being rude.

Fatty did mean to slip out. He had forgotten all about slimming again that day and had eaten too much. He had decided that he would put on his running-shorts and go down to the caravan camp for one last look round – just for luck.

"It's my last chance," he thought. "Goon will be there tomorrow, with his search-warrant – and if there is anything to be found, He'll find it! Blow – blow – BLOW!"

Fatty in Trouble

At about half-past nine Fatty slipped quietly down the stairs, in his singlet and running-shorts. He thought that nobody had heard him, as he went out of the side door.

But the watchful Eunice had not only heard him, but seen him too! She was in her room, with the door a little ajar, and she saw him creeping by. She had put on a short skirt and jersey, and wore her rubber shoes, ready for running too. Her heart beat fast. Fatty might be angry – but she was just going to show him that she could run too – and could outwit him as well!

She went out of the side door like a shadow and heard the click of the little side gate. She ran to it and out into the road. Yes, there was Frederick, running fast. Off went Eunice too!

She soon realized that he was off to the caravan camp,

so it was easy to follow him, without getting too near. A little later they were both in the big field, with the quiet caravans standing about here and there.

Some had lights on. Some hadn't. Fatty made his way to the Fangios' caravan, which was lighted inside. Eunice followed like a shadow. Fatty disappeared under the van and Eunice stood in the shadow of a tree and waited. What was Fatty going to do?

Suddenly the caravan door opened and something shot out, landing near Eunice. She jumped as she felt something soft and warm sliding against her bare legs. It was a cat!

"Dirty little beast!" cried a voice from the caravan. "Stay out there!" The door slammed. The cat mewed pitifully, frightened, and Eunice bent to stroke it. Then something else happened. The caravan door opened again, and someone came down the steps.

"Minnie, Minnie, Minnie!" said a voice. "Poor Minnie! Where are you? Did they kick you and throw you out, the beasts? Minnie, Minnie!"

The cat left Eunice and went over to whoever it was nearby. Eunice stood as still as a mouse. Had Fatty heard all this? She hoped he would be careful, hiding under the caravan. If that was the old woman, she wouldn't be at all pleased to find either Fatty or Eunice there!

Fatty was still under the caravan. He too had heard what had happened. He kept perfectly still, hardly breathing, for on no account must the Fangios know that he was there! He heard someone walking down the steps, and heard the calls of "Minnie, Minnie, Minnie!"

"The old lady after her cat again, I suppose," he thought, and then in alarm he felt the cat against him! That would never do! If it mewed, the old woman would certainly grope under the van for it.

"Minnie, Minnie – oh, you've gone to hide under the van again," said the voice. "Here, puss, here!" And then to Fatty's awful horror, Mrs. Fangio came crawling under the van too. He tried to creep backwards, away from her, but

124

she heard him and in a trice a very hard hand caught hold of his arm.

"Who's this! Who's this!" she cried, and called loudly, "Josef! Lucita! Come here!"

Before they could come, the old lady had dragged Fatty out from under the van, and given him such a box on the ear that he fell over on his side. He could not bring himself to strike back, or even to struggle too hard, for to hit a woman was something Fatty could not do.

And then Josef was on top of him, and Lucita was there with a torch! The cat gave a frightened howl and disappeared.

"It's that boy – the boy who was here before!" hissed Mrs. Fangio, evidently afraid of attracting attention from the nearby vans. "Why does he spy on us? Josef – take him to that old caravan and lock him in. Gag him first. See, here is my shawl."

The shawl was pulled tightly round poor Fatty's face, and somebody tied his arms behind him. Struggling hard, and kicking out, he was half-dragged, half-carried to the smelly old caravan he had peeped into the night before. He was thrown in, and the door was locked.

Fatty was extremely angry. To think that he had been caught as easily as that! But how fierce and strong that old woman was – he felt his ear burning – it was swollen and stinging with the blow she had given it. What a horrid old woman! And yet how gentle she had been with the cat!

Fatty lay still in the smelly caravan, trying to get back his breath. Pooh! The smell nearly made him sick! He lay and thought rapidly. What was he to do? He couldn't shout because he was gagged. He couldn't try to open the door because his arms were tied behind his back. Perhaps he could kick at the door and get help? No – that would bring other caravan folk here, and he might be given a bad time – especially if the Fangios came along too!

And then, as he lay there, he heard an anxious voice outside. "Frederick – are you all right?"

125

Gracious goodness, it was Eunice! Fatty could hardly believe his hears. EUNICE! She must have followed him all the way to the camp. Well – thank goodness she had. Perhaps she could get him out of this mess.

He drummed on the wooden floor with his heels to let her know that he was alive and kicking. He heard her rattling at the door, but it was locked, and there was no key.

Then he heard her climbing up to stand on the wheel to look through the small window. It was broken, but was far too small for her to climb through to help Fatty.

"Frederick – it's me, Eunice," she said.

Fatty could not say anything because of the shawl tied tightly round his mouth, but he drummed hard with his feet again. Eunice shone her torch in at the window and gave a gasp when she saw poor Fatty lying there gagged and bound. "Frederick – listen!" she said. "I'm going to tell you what I think I'd better do. Drum two or three times with your feet if you agree, but only once if you don't."

Fatty heard and drummed thankfully with his feet. Good old Eunice! Now – had she a sensible plan?

"I can't unlock the door and I can't get in at the window," she said. "I'm frightened of trying to get help from the caravan people in case the Fangios interfere and catch me as well. So I'm going to go straight back to your home and get help. Is that all right?"

Fatty drummed vigorously with his feet. Yes, that was fine! Thank goodness she hadn't suggested going to Goon.

"I'll tell your father what has happened and leave it to him to say what's best to do next," said Eunice. "Well, I'm going now, Frederick, though I hate leaving you like this. I shall run all the way. It won't be long before you get help."

Fatty drummed again. What a blessing Eunice had followed him! He heard her jump down from the caravan and then he lay still and began to think about the whole mystery. Those Fangios – where *were* they hiding that man – that second man whose voice he had heard during the quarrel in the caravan? Could there be a false bottom to the van? He hadn't thought of that.

"Well, if there is, Goon will find it in the morning," he thought. "To think that old Goon will at last have solved a mystery before I have!"

He wondered how far Eunice had got. If she ran, it wouldn't take her long to get home and raise the alarm. Probably his father would telephone Chief Inspector Jenks. Well – he wouldn't be very pleased about *that*!

Eunice had shot off through the field to the gate, being careful not to be seen. It was a very dark night, and a mist was coming up from the river. Eunice ran through the gate and away up the road, and then stopped at a corner. She gazed into the mist that was now hiding familiar landmarks.

"Blow! This mist is going to make things difficult," thought Eunice. "Well – I think I turn up here."

And she promptly took the wrong road! She ran on and on, looking for a corner that never came. She stopped at last, and looked round and about fearfully. Where in the world was she?

"*Don't* say I've lost my way!" she groaned. "I'd better ask at some house or other. Blow this mist!"

But there were no houses to be seen! Eunice had taken the path to the river, and now there was nothing but fields. She was on the path beside the river – and as she stood there she heard the water not far off.

She left the path and took a few paces to one side – and stopped with a gasp. Yes – there was the river!

"Well, now I'm *completely* lost!" said poor Eunice. "I don't even know whether to go forward or backward – or turn off to my right. Certainly I can't turn off to the left or I'll be in the river! I wish this mist would clear!"

She tried walking to the right but gave it up and came back to the path again. There was nothing but a field of long wet grass on the right. "I'd better walk straight along the path," decided Eunice. "I'm bound to get somewhere then!"

So off she went, shining her torch in front of her. But she was now on the long, long river-path to Marlow, and it seemed as if the way would go on stretching into the swirling mist for ever and ever. Eunice was almost in tears.

"Just when I have to get help quickly!" she thought, and went on and on. Then she realized that her torch was giving out. The beam it threw was getting faint. She was very frightened then. She might easily walk into the river if her torch no longer lighted her way.

She gave a sudden exclamation. "What's this? An old boat-house! If only I could get in there and wait till daylight! I simply daren't go on with my torch giving out."

It was easy to make her way into the dilapidated old boat-house. There was an old boat there, and Eunice scrambled into it thankfully. She made herself as comfortable as she could with sacks and a rotting tarpaulin.

"Now I must just wait for daylight," she thought. "There's nothing else to do! Oh, *why* did I lose my way when it was so very, very important that I should get help quickly?"

She felt sure that she would not be able to sleep – but in five minutes' time she was fast asleep and dreaming. When she awoke, the daylight was streaming in at the dirty window of the boat-house. Eunice could not for the life of her think where she was!

Then she remembered, and jumped up, stiff and cold. "Oh dear – how could I have slept like that? What's the time? Gracious, it's half-past seven! Poor, poor Fatty – what must he be thinking!"

She made her way out of the boat-house and saw a path running from it across the field beyond. "That's the path to take," she thought, thankfully, and away she went. Soon she was on the outskirts of Peterswood.

She ran up a road, recognizing it as one she had been in before. A little way up a boy and a girl were swinging on a gate, waiting for the postman.

"Why – it's Pip!" said Eunice, thankfully. "And Bets! I'd better tell them what's happened."

Pip was most surprised to see a dirty, tired, most untidy Eunice padding up to his gate. "You *are* out early!" he began, but she interrupted him.

"Pip, listen! Fatty's in trouble. He's lying in a caravan in Barker's Field, gagged and bound. I went to fetch help last night and lost my way in the mist. I'm only just on my way to his house now."

"Good *gracious*!" said Pip, startled. "I'll go and telephone Larry and we'll go down to the field at once. You'd better go on to Fatty's house and give the news there. Whatever happened? Tell me quickly!"

Eunice told her story in a few words and then went off again, not feeling at all happy. Pip and Bets rushed off to telephone Larry. What a thing to happen to poor old Fatty!

The Man with the Scar

Larry was most astonished at Pip's news and very concerned. "I don't see that we can do anything else but go round to old Goon and get him to come with us and set Fatty free," he said, gloomily. "It's maddening, because he'll gloat like anything."

"Yes – and he's going to search the camp this morning for the man with a scar," said Pip, "He'll gloat even more when he finds him – in front of us too, probably! Well, get on your bike, Larry, and meet me at Goon's as quickly as you can."

In four minutes both boys were at Goon's house, knocking at the door. The daily woman, Mrs. Boggs, opened it, surprised to see them so early.

"You can't see Mr. Goon," she said. "He's gone down to the caravan camp with two other constables to do a bit of searching for something. That's all I know. If you want him, you'll have to go there."

"Oh – thank you," said Larry, disappointed. He was just turning away when an idea came to him. "I think I'll telephone Chief Inspector Jenks, Pip," he said. "You know, Goon's spiteful enough to leave Fatty in that caravan for ages, and if there's no key we shan't be able to let him out ourselves."

The woman let them in to telephone, though she wasn't very pleased, and stood over them all the time. Larry could not get on to the Chief himself, who wasn't there, but left an urgent message for him. Then the boys went off to Barker's Field on their bicycles, to find Daisy and Bets awaiting them.

"Goon's here, if you want to speak to him," said Daisy, eagerly. "Which is the caravan that Fatty is in, Larry?"

"I've no idea," said Larry, looking round at the crowd of vans all over the field. "Come on, Pip – we'll just go and tell Goon about Fatty, and make him ask the Fangios for the key."

The caravanners were all in a state of indignation and curiosity. Goon was at his most pompous, ordering people to stand back or to come forward, or to remain where they were. He and the two constables with him had already gone into two or three caravans and searched them thoroughly.

Larry went up to Goon. "Mr. Goon," he said, "we want your help, please. Fatty is locked up in one of these caravans, here – we don't know which – and we want you to get it unlocked and set him free."

Goon was astounded. What! That fat boy actually locked up in one of these vans? Why? Who locked him in? He was just about to ask Larry a few questions when he thought better of it. No. Let that pest of a boy stay locked up as long as possible – until he, Goon, had found the man with a scar, and *then* he'd let Fatty out so that he could watch his triumph. Aha! This would be one time Goon was on top and Fatty was nowhere!

"I can't interrupt my duties," he told Larry, pompously.

130

"I'll see to that fat friend of yours when I've finished the business I'm on. Now clear off!'"

Larry was very angry. "Come on, Pip," he said. "We'll go and find the van ourselves and see if we can't get Fatty out."

They were joined by Daisy and Bets, and quickly made a round of the vans. As practically all the caravan people were out of their vans, standing about talking, and watching Goon and his men, it was easy to tell the two or three caravans in which Fatty might be locked up, for the doors of these were shut.

"This is the one," cried Pip, standing on the wheel of one and looking in through a small broken window. "I can see Fatty – he's lying on the floor, gagged, with his arms tied behind him. Fatty! Poor old Fatty! It won't be long now before we've set you free."

The four children looked at the door. It was old and frail, and the boys felt sure they could break it down. "Come on – all together!" said Larry.

Crash! The door fell from its hinges with hardly any trouble. Larry climbed over it and untied the shawl from Fatty's face, and undid the ropes that bound him. He sat up, looking extremely tired. He worked his arms about to get the stiffness out of them.

"What happened?" he said, and the boys told him how Eunice had lost her way in the mist, and how she had seen Pip when at last she made her way back early that morning. "And that wretch of a Goon's got his search-warrant and is searching the caravans now," ended Pip.

Fatty groaned. "This is a miserable affair, isn't it?" he said. "If that fellow with a scar is in the camp, Goon is sure to find him – and *how* he'll crow over us!"

"Do you want to wait and see who it is?" asked Larry.

Just then Bets heard shouts of excitement coming from the other side of the field and looked out to see what was causing them. "I *say*! she said. "I do believe it's the Chief arriving – with two of his men."

"Whatever for?" said Fatty, in disgust. "Now he'll see
131

Goon on top and us nowhere! Whatever made *him* come?"

"Well – I phoned him," said Larry, rather crestfallen.

"Well, you *are* a fathead," said Fatty. "He's the last person I want to see! I think I'll slip off without speaking to him. I feel pretty awful, and I'm filthy."

"Oh, Fatty, don't look so miserable," said Bets. "Please don't. It's not like you!"

"Right. I won't!" said Fatty, and gave her a rather tired grin. "Come on. Let's go."

They all went down the caravan steps, Fatty finding himself curiously wobbly. "Look – Goon's just got to the Fangios' caravan," said Daisy, thrilled. "Oh, Fatty – do you think they'll find anyone hidden there – rolled up in a mattress or something?"

Josef, Lucita and old Mrs. Fangio had been ordered to come out of their caravan, while it was being searched. Josef went down the steps, looking angry, Lucita seemed scared, and old Mrs. Fangio clutched the cat, and called out something rude in her cackling voice.

Just at that moment Chief Inspector Jenks arrived at the caravan too. Goon was very surprised to see him, and wished suddenly that he had sent to rescue Fatty from the locked caravan.

"No results yet, Chief," said Goon, saluting. "Of course the man with a scar that was reported to us from this camp yesterday may have gone." Then, with a wave of his hand he sent his two helpers to search the Fangios' caravan.

"What's all this about?" cackled old Mrs. Fangio, indignantly. "We ain't done nothing!"

Fatty was standing watching. He was frowning. He remembered that quarrel in the caravan – there *had* been two men there, he knew there had – and certainly Lucita and Mrs. Fangio had been there too. And yet when three people had left the caravan, it had been empty. The fourth person had apparently vanished into thin air! Would the two constables find his hiding-place? As he stared, the two men came down out of the caravan and shook their heads.

"Nothing there," they said.

"Right," said Goon, and turned to the Fangios. "You can go back," he said and the three went up the steps, grumbling among themselves.

It was just at that very moment that something exploded in Fatty's mind, and the whole mystery became as clear as crystal! The man with a scar? Yes, of *course* Fatty knew who it was! How could he have been so blind?

He gave a kind of yelp, and Goon and the Chief turned in surprise. "Why – you're here, Frederick," began the Chief. "How did you m—"

He stopped, for Fatty was gripping his arm fiercely.

"Sir! I can show you the escaped prisoner – the man you want, the man with a scar!" he half-shouted.

"What's this?" said the Chief, astonished. "What do you mean? Where is he?"

"I'll show you!" shouted Fatty, and pushed Goon roughly aside and ran up the caravan steps. Josef and Lucita had gone inside, but the old woman was still at the top, holding the cat and watching the crowd below with a mocking look on her wrinkled, screwed-up face.

Fatty took hold of her arm, gripping it tightly. He snatched at the shawl round Mrs. Fangio's head and ripped it off. Then he grabbed off the dirty white hair – and below it was thick brown hair!

"A wig!" shouted Fatty. "And wipe her face and clean off its painted wrinkles – and you'll find the scar!" He suddenly lunged at the wrinkled face and rubbed the upper lip with the shawl before the old woman could dodge aside. He gave a shout of triumph. "See – the scar is there. Here's your man, Chief, here's . . ."

But the astonished and furious man he held swung round his fist and knocked Fatty off the top of the caravan steps. Then he leapt straight into the watching crowd, sent them flying and raced off, holding up his skirts as he went. The old woman was a man, fierce and strong!

But one of the Chief's men overtook him easily, and,

holding him in a grip of iron, he and the other man frog-marched him to the long black car.

Everyone was so astounded at Fatty's sudden performance that there was quite a silence at first. Then what a hullaballoo! Bets was really frightened.

"Come on, little Bets," said the Chief, picking her up and setting her on his shoulder. "This is no place for you. Goon, you and your men disperse the crowd, please. You can report to me later. Bring in the two Fangios there for questioning."

Lucita began to wail. "We didn't have nothing to do with it! He *made* us help him. He's our cousin and we owe him money, we didn't want to help him, did we, Josef?"

"He's a bad 'un!" shouted Josef. "Always was. You let us alone, we ain't done nothing wrong!"

As Goon seemed to be struck helpless with surprise, the two men he had with him made the Fangios come down, and then took them off, howling and shouting. Everyone followed.

The four children followed too, with Bets on the Chief's shoulder. The first prisoner was now in the big black car, shouting something very loudly out of the window.

"What's he saying?" said the Chief, puzzled. "Something about a *cat*?"

"Yes," said Fatty. "He's yelling 'Somebody look after that cat, somebody look after that cat!' Little does he know that it was the cat that gave his secret away!"

"I must have a little talk with you, Frederick," said the Chief. "Your performance was truly dramatic – but was it necessary to give it just then? Couldn't you have let me know the facts *quietly*?"

"No, sir, I couldn't," said Fatty. "I only knew them my-self at that very moment. They came on me like a flash! I'd like to tell you about it, sir. Can you come back home with us, and I'll make my report?"

"I think I'd better," said the Chief. "My word, you gave Goon the shock of his life when you ended the whole thing so dramatically. He almost fainted with surprise!"

Fatty looked back over his shoulder. Goon was staring after him, his mouth open, and his helmet decidedly crooked.

"I expect he's saying 'Gah!'," said Bets. "He looks like it. Poor old Goon – he might so easily have solved the mystery first."

"Look – there's Eunice – and Buster," said Fatty, suddenly. "Gosh – and my father and mother too! I hope Eunice didn't scare them too much when she got home and told them I was locked up in a van!"

"Frederick – what *is* the meaning of all this?" said Mr. Trotteville, looking anxious and upset. "Eunice came home with such a tale – oh, good morning, Chief, you here too! What in the wide world has been happening?"

"Well, sir, if you'd allow me to come back with you, I've a few questions to ask Frederick here," said the Chief, politely. "I'm really as much in the dark as you are."

"Yes, yes – come back by all means," said Mrs. Trotteville. "Frederick, have you had any breakfast?"

"No. Nobody has," said Fatty, cheerfully, patting a most excited Buster. "Except the Chief. I expect he's had his, haven't you, Chief?"

"I certainly have," said the Chief. "Ah, I see you have a car – good. Will it take us all?"

"*We've* got our bikes," said Larry. "We'll bike up as quickly as we can. See you later!"

Well Done, Fatty!

Jane was most amazed to see so many arriving for breakfast. She and Cookie began to fry eggs and bacon at top speed and to make pieces of toast.

Eunice found a moment to have a word with Fatty. She

looked very downcast. "I lost my way last night," she said. "I'm awfully sorry, Frederick. I went for miles and miles in the mist!"

"Never mind!" said Fatty, grinning. "It'll take a bit of your fat off, Eunice. Cheer up!"

"Well, now, Frederick, would you like to tell me what led up to your truly remarkable performance this morning?" asked the Chief when breakfast was on the table. He sat down in a chair and took out his notebook. "Right from the time when I first informed you of the man with a scar, and asked you to keep an eye open for him."

"Well, sir – there were a whole lot of odd *clues* – but none of them seemed to fit together," said Fatty. "I mean, we spotted the likeness of the Fangios to the photo of the scarred man – but you told us he'd got no relations – and *They* said they'd only got their old mother. . . ."

"Yes. Actually he's a cousin," said the Inspector, "as no doubt you heard the twin Fangios calling out this morning. A cousin they're ashamed of and afraid of. That explains the likeness between them that you were clever enough to spot."

"Yes. That was really the beginning of it all," said Fatty. "Well, quite a lot of things seemed to be clues after that. I mean – the insects, such as the fleas and the beetles. Mrs. Fangio was mixed up with both, so I just thought that a love of insects was in the family, so to speak. Another clue was that they all behaved queerly when I asked them if they knew a man with a scar. That's what made me think of going down to the caravan camp where they lived, and having a look round."

"Excellent idea," said the Chief. "Go on."

"Well, there were other clues, sir – clues that I didn't really recognize," said Fatty. "Large carpet slippers, for instance. I saw Mrs. Fangio wearing them, but didn't imagine that they were really her own – I mean, *his* own – I just thought the old woman had borrowed them from Josef. I didn't guess that they meant that a very large foot was inside them – the foot of a man, not an old woman! And

136

then there was the quarrel in the caravan, when I heard *two* men's voices – and yet only one man was there! And I just didn't have the sense to fit the second voice on to somebody who *was* there – I couldn't understand why there were only three people when there *should* have been a fourth! Of course the *second* man's voice belonged to old Mrs. Fangio, who was using her – I mean his – proper man's voice in the quarrel! She usually put on a sort of cackling old woman's voice!"

"All very complicated for you!" said the Chief. "I can quite see how puzzling everything must have been. Anything else?"

"Yes – the cat," said Fatty, ruefully. "I forgot the scarred man was fond of cats. Actually I thought it was perfectly natural for an old woman like Mrs. Fangio to be fond of the cat, especially when the others were cruel to it. I was blind! I got all the clues and I never saw what they added up to!"

"She even had knobbly hands," put in Bets, "and we noticed them specially!"

"And I never thought of how easily a wrinkle could disguise a scar," groaned Fatty. "Of course, I see now that she – he, I mean – was very clever at disguising himself, and even kept his face all screwed up, so that the false wrinkles and real ones couldn't be distinguished."

"He's known to be a master at disguise," said the Chief, "if that's any comfort to you!"

"Well, it is a bit," said Fatty. "But after all – *I'm* pretty good at disguising myself too, sir. I ought to have seen through his."

"What made you *suddenly* see through Mrs. Fangio?" asked Pip. "I mean – one moment you were as castdown as anything – and the next you were yelling like mad, and tearing up the caravan steps!"

"I don't quite know," said Fatty. "It seemed as if all the muddle of clues in my mind about fleas and beetles and carpet slippers and voices and quarrels and the cat and wrinkles and knobbly hands fell into place – oh yes, *and* something else, sir! Of course! That's what *really* made it click!"

"What?" said everyone, eagerly.

"Well – old Mrs. Fangio, as I thought she was, knocked me right over two nights ago," said Fatty. "I thought it was just a lucky blow on her part. And last night she boxed my ear, hit me on the side of my head – you can see my swollen ear now, sir. And it was a *man's* blow, not a woman's. I remember thinking that at the time, without even guessing it *was* a blow from a man! But my ear began to sting like anything as I stood looking up at the three Fangios on that caravan step this morning – and it was *that* that made everything click into place. I thought: 'It was a *man's* fist that gave me this swollen ear,' and then I knew I was right, and suddenly the whole mystery was solved."

"Oh, Frederick – your poor ear," said his mother. "I must bathe it for you."

"Please don't fuss, Mother," said Fatty. "I'm PROUD of this ear. Well, Chief – I think that's about all. But gosh – I thought old Goon was going to win this time! I just got in by the skin of my teeth."

"Well, my congratulations, Frederick," said the Inspector, standing up. "And, as I think I have said before, I am looking forward to having you on my staff some time in the future – and if anyone gives you a swollen ear then, it will be me, not Mrs. Fangio!"

And away he went with the six children and Buster to see him off.

"I want a bit more breakfast," said Fatty, returning to the dining-room.

"Oh, Frederick – you've forgotten you're slimming!" said Eunice. Fatty gave a determined snort.

"Today is to be a day of celebration, my dear Eunice!" he said. "Buns, lemonade and ice-cream at eleven. A good lunch in the middle of the day. A smashing tea at the best cake-shop in Peterswood – and oh, by the way, what about that cat?"

138

"What cat?" said Eunice.

"The Fangios' cat!" cried Bets. "Oh, of course! They won't want it, poor thing. We'll fetch it, Fatty."

"And it shall have the time of its life because it helped us to solve the Mystery of the Missing Man!" finished Fatty. "What do you say to that, Buster?"

"Wuff," said Buster, and wagged his tail vigorously. "WUFF!"

PONY BOOKS

Do you like pony books? Have you ever tried them? They can be wonderfully exciting, and pony books now have tremendous sales among young people. In fact, after Enid Blyton stories, we sell more books about ponies than on any other subject.

In the Dragon series we have some wonderful pony books. Possibly the most loved is the story of Flicka. This is a magnificently long story, and the opening book is called *My Friend Flicka Part I*.

It is the story of a ranch in Wyoming, and of a boy who is given a pony. But that pony is a descendant of the wild horses that roam the range, and this brings heart-ache to the young owner; for Flicka is intractable for a long time and will not show affection.

The story – which has been read by millions all round the world – tells of the life of the wild horses: of summers that are happy for them, out there in the sun-lit mountains; of winters that are cruelly harsh. It also tells absorbingly of the life of the roaming herds of wild horses, of the fights by stallions to win the leadership of these herds for themselves. The Flicka books are exciting, heartwarming, and often they will move you to tears. Do decide now to buy the first of the Flicka series next time you go to your bookshop or newsagent.

Another series about horses in Dragon books is about the brumbies (wild horses) of Australia. There are four in this series, the first being entitled *The Silver Brumby*.

Again we have a pony series which might be described as a classic. Again we live with wild horses, with most men's hands turned against them, only wanting to be free and to be allowed to roam the wild wide acres without molestation.

Finally, we have excellent pony books by Gillian Baxter and Christine Pullein-Thompson. Delightful stories which have been big selling for months. Why not start to collect your own pony library? The books are not expensive and in very little time you would have a bright array of titles you could be proud of. Make a resolution to buy a Dragon pony book a week!

DRAGON BOOKS

The Dragon series is one of the finest Children's Libraries in print today. Enid Blyton, Lewis Carroll, Lady Antonia Fraser, Noel Streatfeild, Christine Pullein-Thompson, Mary O'Hara, show-jumper Pat Smythe and many others are all here to delight every child, whatever the mood or time of day. The Dragon authors represent a charming array of the most creative and time-honoured talents ever at work in the children's field – a pasture of absorbing and intimate pleasure through which wind our chequered Pied Pipers with their ageless tunes and tales, to the joy of millions of Dragon readers. As for Kid's Power – Dragon Books are just the thing to occupy young people finding out perhaps for the first time that peace and quiet can be lovely with a book, and who are beginning to discover for themselves the surprising fun in store for them in the world beyond the family.

If you or your parents have trouble in obtaining titles, please remember that they are available from Cash Sales Dept., P.O. Box 11, Falmouth, Cornwall, at the price shown plus 7p postage.

ENID BLYTON (cont.)

Fifteen-Minute Tales 20p
Twenty-Minute Tales 20p
More Twenty-Minute Tales 20p
Eight O'Clock Tales 20p
The Children's Life of Christ 17p
The Red Storybook 20p
The Yellow Storybook 20p
The Blue Storybook 20p
The Green Storybook 20p
Tales from the Bible 17p

MARY O'HARA

My Friend Flicka – Part 1 20p
My Friend Flicka – Part 2 20p
Thunderhead – Part 2 12p
Thunderhead – Part 3 12p
Green Grass of Wyoming – Part 1 12p
Green Grass of Wyoming – Part 2 12p
Green Grass of Wyoming – Part 3 12p

CHRISTINE PULLEIN-THOMPSON

The Open Gate 17p
The Empty Field 17p
The First Rosette 17p
The Second Mount 17p
The Pony Dopers 12p
For Want of a Saddle 20p
The Impossible Horse 20p

MOLLIE CLARKE
(In Colour)

Rabbit and Fox *and* Skillywidden 25p
Mink and the Fire
and Aldar the Trickster 25p

PAT SMYTHE

A Swiss Adventure 20p
A Spanish Adventure 20p

ANTONIA FRASER

King Arthur and the Knights of the
  Round Table (Illus. by Rebecca
  Fraser) 40p

LEWIS CARROLL

Alice's Adventures in Wonderland
  (Original illus.) 25p
Alice's Adventures Through the
  Looking-Glass (Original illus.) 25p

ARTHUR C. CLARKE
Dolphin Island 12p

NOEL STREATFEILD
The House in Cornwall 17p

...and many, many more. Enquire at your local bookshop.